RODEO KING

CiCi Cordelia

We'd like to dedicate Rodeo King to all our readers,

for their encouragement and support.

We couldn't do this without you!

Acknowledgment

To our BFF, Callie Hutton. We love you, girl.

Write on!

Chapter One

Caleb carefully stood, trying not to put too much pressure on
his aching leg. He tipped his well-worn Stetson to the young girl
sitting with her grandmother in the seat across from him.

"It's been a pleasure, ma'am," he said solemnly.

The little cutie had talked his ear off the entire way to Dustin,
Wyoming; all seven hours. Her sweet chatter helped keep him from
dwelling on his potentially career-ending fall as a professional bull
rider, and the two months of rehabilitation afterward.

Now the memory pushed to the forefront, and locking his jaw
he stepped off the bus and shoved down the anger that still roared
hot and bright inside him.

Crawling home with my tail between my legs.

How the mighty had fallen. From King of the Rodeo to
washed up cowboy by the age of twenty-eight.

He glanced up and down Main Street, lit only by streetlights
and the signs from nearby businesses as night settled in, and
wondered if Rosemary still lived here. He hadn't heard that she'd
moved or anything. His heart thudded hard against his ribs at the
thought of seeing her again.

He'd taken notice of her when she was fourteen and budding
into womanhood. She'd been a sweet little thing, with a kind heart
and a quick smile. And she'd had a crush on him. But being three
years younger, as well as his buddy's baby sister, and knowing

Mason would kick his ass if he touched her, Caleb had kept his distance.

Then, as her body filled out, Rosemary Carmichael had every cowboy in town salivating for a taste. Jealousy had eaten at him, but he'd been determined not to give in to his desire for her, already knowing he'd be leaving town for bigger things.

At twenty, so cocksure of himself, he'd headed out of town to find fame as a bull rider. And he'd been doing just fine until three years later, during a break from the rodeo circuit, he'd come home for a visit and ended up taking Rosemary to bed. He knew it wasn't a smart move on his part. But he'd wanted her like a starving man wanted a nice juicy steak.

And like a bastard, he'd seduced her, even knowing she wasn't some buckle bunny he could just screw and walk away from.

At least not with a clear conscience.

Images of Rosemary in his bed, naked and trembling with desire as he'd introduced her to the pleasures of sex, flashed across his mind. Barely nineteen, she'd been the hottest girl in town, with a bold attitude for life and huge amber eyes that turned molten gold when she came.

How in the hell was I supposed to know she was a virgin?

Caleb's body tightened even as guilt filtered through him, like it always did when he thought about Rosemary, and their short time together. He swallowed hard, remembering the way her fiery red hair hung loose around her slender shoulders, the sexy sway of her perfect breasts as she sat astride him. She'd been a quick study, and during the week he'd held her in his arms, Caleb had been tempted to stay, whispering sweet promises in her ear.

Then reality set in, and the fact that he even wanted to stay and give up his dreams scared the mother lovin' shit out of him. And like a thief in the night, he'd left without so much as a kiss goodbye.

Even now, six years later, guilt burned through him with the destruction of a blowtorch.

And he still wanted her. Had wanted her since the day he left, never able to completely shut her out of his mind.

"Caleb Johnson, is that you?" a woman's voice called out.

He turned to see Charlotte MacDonald crossing the dusty street with her husband, Mac. Even in the dim lighting, Caleb spotted the look of disapproval on the older woman's face as she and Mac headed his way.

Damn. He'd just gotten off the bus. What could have her panties in a bunch already?

Caleb set his suitcase down and tipped his hat. "Hello, ma'am. Mac."

"Hi, Caleb." Mac was smiling as they neared. "What's brought you back our way?"

Charlotte waved a finger under his nose before he could answer. "It's about time, young man. You should be ashamed of yourself, running off that way!"

Running off? His brows arched. Had Rosemary told folks what happened between them? Yeah, it'd been a crappy thing to do, but the Rosemary he remembered wasn't the type to blast her personal life to any of Dustin's town gossips.

Before he could respond, Mac cut in. "Now, Charlotte, leave the boy be." He offered an apologetic shrug and took his wife's hand, tugging her away. "Glad you're back, Caleb. I think you'll find some things have changed since you left." Mac's soft chuckle followed in his wake as he swept his wife down the street. Charlotte managed to shoot Caleb one more glare over her shoulder before they disappeared around the corner.

What the hell was that about?

He shook his head, reaching down to rub his throbbing leg. The doctors told him he'd get full mobility back, but it was too soon to tell if he'd ever be able to ride again. Caleb was still mulling that over, wondering what he'd do if the worst happened and his career was over before ever really getting started. He loved bull riding, and eight years wasn't nearly long enough. He wasn't sure he could give it up.

Would I really have a choice?

Caleb flicked a glance toward the Bronco Inn, two blocks down from the bus station. Since his folks had moved away shortly after he'd graduated high school, a temporary place to stay was first on his agenda. He'd grab some food, then get a room for the night and start apartment hunting. He'd managed to save up a considerable nest egg, enough to tide him over for a while.

Even though he was loath to admit it, he knew the reason he'd chosen to come back to Dustin was because of Rosemary. They had unfinished business. She was like a burr under his saddle he couldn't dislodge. Maybe if he had another taste or two of her, he could get her out of his system and move on.

Maybe.

He just hoped she was still here.

As he walked down the mostly deserted streets, everyone inside drinking, having dinner, or shopping, with a few stragglers wandering about, he glanced at his watch. Six-thirty. There'd be time to catch a bite and a beer before grabbing a room. He might look up Mason. Word was his old buddy still lived here, and had the veterinary clinic he'd always dreamed of.

Good for him.

A tight knot curled in Caleb's gut. He should have kept in contact with Mason, but he'd let their friendship fall away after sleeping with the man's sister. He raked his fingers through his hair and blew out a strained breath.

When did I become such a bastard? But he knew. It was the moment he'd slipped from Rosemary's bed and hightailed it out of town.

Now in serious need of a drink, Caleb hoofed it down the street, albeit at a slow pace, toward the local brewpub. It was a warm, muggy evening and his shirt stuck to his back as he approached the pub. He licked his dry lips, eager to taste the cold brew. As he headed up the sidewalk, a door flew open a few buildings from the pub, and a man stepped out, calling his name.

Caleb turned slightly and recognized Mason standing just outside the door under a sign lettered with 'Mason's Veterinary Service.'

He set his suitcase down again. "Damn, Carmichael," he said, grinning, "how the hell are you, man?"

Mason's expression darkened ominously and Caleb lost his smile.

Well, I guess that answers that question.

When Mason came toward him with murder in the tense lines of his body, Caleb didn't even try to defend himself as the man brought his fist back and swung at him. He deserved the beat-down he was about to take. It wasn't a glancing blow and pain radiated through his jaw as he fell onto his ass. His Stetson flew off his head and landed on the sidewalk.

He stared up at his former friend as he fingered his jaw, rotating it to see if it was broken. It wasn't. Not yet, anyway. "Feel better?"

Mason stormed toward him, reaching down to grip the front of his shirt, and jerked him to his feet. The movement sent fire shooting through Caleb's leg and he gritted his teeth against the pain.

"Not by a long shot, you son of a bitch." Mason reared back to punch him again.

Caleb narrowed his eyes, but didn't fight back, although anger bent the edges of his control. He'd let Mason get in a few more punches before he defended himself. It was the least he could do after sleeping with his pal's baby sister.

But Caleb's patience only went so far . . .

"Mason. Stop!" The feminine voice shot across the semi-darkness and both men froze.

Mason glared at him. "You have no goddamn idea what you did, do you, asshole?"

Caleb couldn't help it as images of making love to Rosemary flooded his mind. He chuckled. "I've got a pretty good idea."

Yep. He really did deserve the next punch Mason threw his way, reconnecting with his aching jaw and sending him back a few feet, though he managed to remain standing. The force of the blow made him bite hard on the inside of his cheek.

"Mason, no!" Rosemary rushed toward them.

A different woman's voice called from the same direction. "Hit him harder next time, Mason."

Caleb spat blood. "Are we done?"

"Not even close," Mason growled.

Rosemary grabbed her brother's arm and tugged. "Mason, don't, damn it."

Caleb shifted his gaze to Rosemary, and every muscle in his body seized along with his breath, as she flipped her long, wavy hair over one shoulder. She was even more beautiful than he remembered. He wanted to bury his hands in those thick red locks and take her sweet mouth in a kiss. Her heart-shaped face held a healthy freshness, her lips plump and rosy, but her figure now fully a woman's, generously curved in all the right places.

Fucking perfection.

His body responded to her lush beauty, just like it always had, and he was thankful for the dim light as he shifted slightly to relieve the pressure under his button fly.

Another woman he recognized from high school had come up behind her, but he couldn't recall her name. A little boy held her hand, his small frame tucked against her leg.

Regret filled him. They were fighting in front of a kid. He turned back to Rosemary, ignoring her brother completely. "Hi," he said softly, his heart pounding fast.

Her mouth tightened. She didn't act happy to see him, and rather than return his greeting, she glanced up at her brother. "Let's just go."

Go? Hell, no! Caleb didn't want her to leave, he just wanted to stare at her a little longer. She was like candy to his soul and he was starving for her. By the hard expression on her face, she didn't want a damn thing to do with him.

And who could blame her?

Dickhead! What had he been thinking, walking away from this woman?

Mason's posture relaxed as he glanced over to the woman and little boy. *His kid?* Caleb hadn't heard about Rosemary's brother getting hitched or anything.

"Mommy, can we go home now?" the boy asked in a soft voice.

"In a moment, sweetheart," Rosemary replied gently.

Caleb's world went black, and for a moment he couldn't breathe as his legs shook beneath him, the implication of what just happened like a crowbar to the kneecaps.

He turned toward the little boy, peeking out from behind the woman who still held his hand. Inhaling sharply, Caleb stared into eyes that mirrored his own, a child wearing his face and shocking red hair like his mother's.

His son.

Chapter Two

With a soft, despairing moan, Rosemary Carmichael registered pain she'd thought long buried. Those hot green eyes hadn't changed a bit, and they were focused on Carson. Her innocent baby, who looked far too much like his daddy despite the red hair he'd inherited from her.

She'd been young, in love, and stupid as well, to think Caleb Johnson would ever settle down in a two-bit place like Dustin. He'd been too talented and already too well-known, riding bulls like nobody's business and winning every local and then state championship the Wyoming rodeo circuit could offer. But God, she'd wanted him. And she'd had him for one short, soul-destroying week.

Hungrily, she drank him in from the top of his tangled, dark blond hair to the tarnished tips of his battered Dan Posts. A pair of faded-out Levi's rode low on lean hips she could recall gripping in the throes of a passion that could still break her out in a sweat to think on, all these years later. His denim shirt was just as faded, creased from travel, the sleeves rolled up to his elbows. The pale blue fabric strained against the breadth of his shoulders and whipcord muscles she knew he'd honed during years on the pro rodeo circuit. He looked bigger, more powerful, more intimidating. Sexier than hell.

Yet she wanted to slap the shock right off his darkly tanned face; wanted to scoop up her child and run a thousand miles away.

Until she couldn't see the way his full lips had begun to form the question she sure as shit didn't want to answer—

"Mine?" The rough gravel in his voice made her swallow nervously, which got her anger cooking at the guilt trying to rear up and smother her.

I've got nothing to be guilty about. Rosemary jerked her chin high, her lips pursed in annoyance. "Mine."

Caleb's jaw clenched. One wide, long-fingered hand reached for his stained hat and he slapped it against his leg before dropping it back on his head.

Damn it, nobody in the world had the right to look that sinful in a black, worn-down Stetson. The instant she thought it, Rosemary squelched it. She wasn't nineteen any longer.

"Tell me whose boy this is." Caleb obviously wasn't going to back down, which she knew would piss her brother off.

Sure enough, Mason reacted predictably, stepping close to Caleb and bumping boot-tips with him. The similarities between her brother and the man she'd given everything to almost brought a smile to her face. Both of them handsome, tough, tall, broad. Intimidating. And best friends no longer. *My fault.* The words hovered, fueling fresh heartache.

As Carson huddled closer to Susan Lewis, honorary aunt and Rosemary's best friend since first grade, Mason's lip curled in his customary sneer. "None of your fucking business. You lost those kinds of rights when you took off." He leaned in, lifted a hand and flicked at Caleb's Stetson, deliberately knocking it off. It spun once and landed back on the ground, brim-up.

Caleb's face darkened. "You son of a—"

"Susie-Q, take Carson home, okay?" Rosemary broke in as calmly as possible, certain Susan's temper could blow at any second. Her hair might not be red, but when she went into 'aunty' mode, nobody was more protective.

For a second she thought Susan would explode anyway, because she had that look in her pale blue eyes that usually meant her claws were out and ready to shred skin. But her arm curled closer around Carson's small, sturdy body and she nodded, sending jet-black corkscrew curls sliding over one shoulder.

"Come on, Lil' Tuff." She gently led him away, Carson turning with a gap-toothed grin and one hand waving in Rosemary's direction. Off they skipped, her boy's high, sweet chatter floating on the air along with Susan's deeper chuckle.

Blinking back a sudden sting of tears, Rosemary turned, and met Caleb's piercing stare. A feeling of unease swept over her.

"Carson. You named him after my granddad." It wasn't a question.

She fought the need to slump in defeat, instead stiffening her spine. "Mason, can you take off for a bit? I need—I need to talk to Caleb." She shot her brother a 'don't-say-anything-more' look.

He visibly bristled. "Not smart, Rosie." He folded his arms across his chest and loomed close, overprotective as usual.

"I've got things I need to say, Mason. It'll be all right," she assured him. "Come on. Give me a little breathing room. You can be the big bro tomorrow." Her gaze locked with his, eyes the same deep amber as hers.

Mason huffed in anger and turned to face down Caleb, who'd collected his hat off the ground and was brushing dirt off the crown. "If you make her cry, I'll make you suffer." Both hands fisted, he stomped off to catch up with Susan and Carson.

His expression visibly bleak, Caleb watched as Mason took Carson's other hand and walked away, her son gleefully jumping and swinging between two of his favorite people.

Rosemary swallowed the choking lump of emotion lodged in her throat and gestured toward one of the wooden benches the Chamber of Commerce had installed around Dustin a few years back. "Okay, ask your questions." She perched on the edge, ready to jump and run, uncomfortable at the thought of sharing a seat with him.

But Caleb remained standing, shoving his hands in his back pockets. For a moment he stared off down the street, before turning and pinning her in place with a narrow gaze. "I want to know why you never told me."

She hunched a shoulder in a defensive shrug. "Nobody knew where you were."

"That's bullshit! Uncle Zip knew. I asked him to tell your daddy."

"Zip left town about three days after you did, Caleb." She gestured wearily. "And my daddy told me nothing. After he moved to Cody, Mama lost touch, probably on purpose. You know they only stayed together for Mason and me."

The words coated her tongue with bitterness, forcing her to recall how her folks fought, in public as well as in private. "The day after you left, Daddy punched out Zip and accused him of trying to romance my mama. Zip laughed in his face and took off. Then Daddy and Mama started really fighting, and it never got any better. He skipped town before Carson was born, and ended up in Cody. He's got the John Deere franchise up there. Seems happy, but he's only seen Carson a few times over the years. And that's fine by me."

"You could have found out where I was, easily enough," Caleb began, but she cut him off.

"I woke up and you were gone. For God's sake, you left in the middle of the night like you were ashamed of me! No email address . . . I wrote you several times and sent the letters out General Delivery to the State Rodeo Commission. They came back, 'addressee unknown.' Once you started making it big on the circuit, I searched the internet a few times for whatever I could find on you. But I gave up on that, too. As far as I was concerned, we were done."

Her temples had started to throb with an oncoming headache. The pain made her cranky as hell, and Rosemary found she'd reached the end of her patience. She snapped, "You didn't leave me a thing. Not a note, not a phone number. Nothing. Just a clump of

cowshit on the carpet from those damned rands you liked to wear."
She jerked a thumb at the scarred-up silver trim on his boot heels. "I
see you still wear them."

"Don't change the subject." His voice had risen, attracting
attention from a few folks wandering in and out of the brewpub.

She stifled a sigh. The town had been nosy ever since she
could remember, and trying to keep a secret was as much a wasted
effort now as it'd been years ago when she first peed on a pregnancy
stick and burst into tears when two blue lines appeared. Within a few
months everyone in Dustin knew she was carrying Caleb Johnson's
baby, including her furious daddy and sad-eyed, disappointed mama.
Time had made some things better, and other things worse.

"Look," she reasoned, "there isn't a thing I can do about
what happened years ago. You screwed me senseless for a week and
then you left—"

"Stop talking like that!" he protested. "What we had meant
more than a week of screwing around."

"No. It didn't. I stopped kidding myself a long time ago,
Caleb. Around the same time I found out how much it cost to raise a
baby." She pressed chilled fingers to her temples. "Mama didn't
really forgive me for months, and Daddy never got over it. All he
could see was the way history repeated itself, that I'd done the same
thing as Mama, upped and got myself pregnant. Difference was,
Mama made my daddy come home and marry her, so Mason would
be legitimate. I found out real fast how hard it is being a single

parent." She shook her head. "I don't know what I would have done without Mason to help me get on my feet."

"Damn it, I would never have abandoned my son," Caleb growled, stepping closer to the bench.

Rosemary quaked with fresh anger, but held herself steady. "I'm not saying that, you dumb cowboy. I've got a good job at the credit union and a place of my own, so I'm supporting him just fine. I even make Mama accept a little babysitting money whenever she takes him while I'm at work. I've got a savings account building up and Carson's happy. It's all that matters." She dropped into a low, serious rasp. *"He's all that matters."*

She jumped off the bench before Caleb could react to her words. Rosemary pushed her heavy hair out of her face and took little satisfaction at the way Caleb watched her, as if starved for her. It made no difference, because he wouldn't stay. She'd spotted how he favored his leg, and figured an injury had sidelined him. But he'd be gone again as soon as his leg mended. Rodeo was in his blood. In his soul. There wasn't room for anything else, and she'd been an idiot once to imagine she could change him.

She'd grown up a hell of a lot since then.

"I have to go. It's Carson's bedtime soon and he'll want a story." She turned away, but Caleb grabbed her arm.

"I want to get to know him."

Yanking her arm from his grasp, Rosemary spun and shoved a hard finger in his chest. "He has a name. And you have no rights, other than being a sperm donor. You gave up those rights when you snuck out of my bed after popping my cherry. Hell, Caleb, I didn't even warrant a goodbye. Just 'slam, bam, thank you ma'am,' then you were gone. How do you think that made me feel?"

She darted past him, and this time Caleb made no move to stop her. When she glanced back, he stood there like a chunk of stone, and from the short distance between them she could read stark misery on his handsome face. It would have broken her heart if she'd had anything left to break. But what she'd felt inside for him had been sliced into pieces a long time ago.

"Rosie."

Hearing her childhood nickname on Caleb's lips did an emotional number on her, but she schooled her face to utter calm as she spun back around on a boot heel. "What, Caleb?"

"I'm . . ." He paused and rubbed his hand over his jaw. "Hell. I'm sorry. I really want to get to know my son. Please, Rosemary. I just want to be around him a little."

The tears she'd held back all evening spilled down her cheeks, but she wouldn't wipe them away. Rosemary stood tall and replied hoarsely, "I need to think on it some, all right? Just let me—let me think."

She didn't want to act like a selfish bitch. She sure as hell didn't want to hold anything over Caleb's head the way her mama had done to Daddy. She and Mason had grown up in a shaky, uncertain household, privy to hourly bickering, daily arguments and the kind of knock-down-drag-outs no kid should have to endure. All because their father had felt trapped in a loveless marriage, and their mother had tried to hold on to her husband with guilt and duty. To this day Mason had a strong aversion to a serious commitment, and Rosemary would probably go to her grave unsure of whether her birth had been an attempt at reconciliation or just another accidental pregnancy.

What kind of life was that for a little kid?

No way. She'd never do that. For the sake of her son she'd pulled herself together, mended the broken bits, and given all of them to Carson.

Unable to stand there much longer and not break down completely, she fled.

She had nothing left for the King of the Rodeo.

Chapter Three

Stepping up to the Bronco Inn's registration desk, Caleb dinged the little bell sitting on the counter. After a minute or so, the pocket door separating the lobby from what was the living quarters of the owners slid back as Nash Gardner stepped out, wiping his mouth on a handkerchief.

"Hey, Nash." Caleb nodded to him.

"Johnson." Nash tossed the handkerchief aside. "What can I do you for?"

Nash had been a couple of grades ahead of him in school, raised on state welfare. Caleb was impressed at how the guy had dug himself out from the crap side of town and bought The Bronco Inn.

Caleb leaned his elbows on the glass-covered counter. Nash had made a decent motel out of a mere skeleton, no mean feat. While the rooms wouldn't win any awards, they were clean and reasonable, with comfortable beds and showers that didn't smell like mildew. But after only two days, Caleb was already feeling claustrophobic and needed a bigger place. "That apartment complex over on Dart still up and running?"

Nash scratched at his goatee. "Far as I know." He pondered for a moment, staring at Caleb. "How long you thinkin' of hanging around? I got a bigger room set up as a studio. Full bath. Living room. Even got a kitchenette with a stove and a decent sized fridge. More than enough for one person. I rent it by the week or month. It's empty right now. I can show you."

"Yeah?" Caleb's interest was piqued by a month-to-month agreement. Most apartment leases tried to lock you into six months, minimum. Hell, he didn't have a clue what might happen, between his healing leg and the question of going back on the circuit. Not to mention Rosemary. *And the boy.*

Nash opened a drawer and extracted a key with an oblong room number tag attached. He slid it across the counter. "Tell you what. My food's getting cold and I want to finish eating. Go take a look for yourself. All the way to the end. Number Fourteen. I can give you a weekly deal to start." He named a figure that was only a few bucks higher than what Caleb had paid on Room Five for the last few nights, total.

"Okay, I will. Thanks, buddy." Caleb crossed to the door.

"Wait a sec." Nash called him back. When Caleb turned, Nash was holding up another set of keys. "If you're gonna stay more'n a week or two, I got a truck you can borrow now and then. It's kind of beat up but it runs good. That little red Dodge on the back lot." He jerked his chin toward a side exit. "I don't need it and you know a truck's gotta be driven or else the engine ends up choked. Just keep it filled with gas and we're square." He hung the set of keys in a wall cabinet that had a small press-button lock. "Combo's three-six-ten-five."

"Nash, that's really generous, but I—"

"Use it when you need it, Johnson." Nash regarded him soberly. "You helped me out some, years ago. Loaned me money a couple of times and never asked for nothing back. I'm glad to return the favor." He cocked his head to the side and gestured toward Caleb's face with a sudden grin. "That jaw's lookin' better. Nice and yellow instead of black and blue."

"Kiss my ass, Gardner."

Nash rasped out a guffaw, then nodded sharply. "Got to finish my meal. Let me know if you want the studio." He disappeared behind the pocket door, sliding it shut behind him.

Caleb stood for a few seconds, undecided. He hated being beholden to anyone, but Nash's offer of a vehicle was too good to pass up. Dustin was small enough that he could walk just about anywhere he needed, even on a bum leg. Still, the truck would come in handy once in a while.

Heading out the front door, he sought out Fourteen. The two-room unit wasn't grand, but it was spotlessly clean and functional. He could relax in here and map out his time in Dustin. Figure out what to do about Rosemary. She'd been avoiding him the last couple days and he'd let her, not yet ready to face her.

His plan had been simple when he'd decided to return. A short-term lease, something he could get out of when his leg was healed enough to climb back onto a bucking bull. It was supposed to be easy. Check into town, see if Rosemary was still around, then head back out to the circuit when the time was right. Maybe even taking her along for the ride if things worked out.

Staring into the eyes of his son had thrown that out the window.

Caleb crossed to the door and stepped outside, resigned to taking the studio. The weekly rent sure wouldn't break him, and he'd be able to spread out some. At least enough until he figured out what the hell he was going to do now.

An hour later he'd moved his stuff over from the other room and shoved a few things into the highboy drawers; hung up some shirts. A fast shower and shave made him feel more human, and he relaxed on the loveseat with a cold longneck in one hand and the TV remote in the other, flipping through channels.

The world was still in chaos, the local cops were trying to find the kids who scrawled curse words on the school building, and the weather was cool, but seasonal.

And he was a father. If that didn't just blow his ever-lovin' mind!

"A son." He said the word aloud, trying to wrap his head around it. *Carson.* The same as his grandfather. Even after the way he'd acted, Rosemary had thought about him when she named their son. That had to mean something . . .

A loud growl from his stomach reminded him he hadn't eaten in hours. What he needed now was a burger and another beer. Caleb slapped his hat on his head, pocketed the room key, and headed out.

Five minutes later, he pushed open the door to DeeDee's, the first sense of true welcome to hit him since he'd gotten off the bus two days ago. He hardly counted Mason Carmichael's punch to his face a welcome.

He headed straight to the bar area and grabbed a table, then gestured to the burly bartender, busy polishing glasses. "Hey, Mikey, get me a Bud."

"That you, Johnson?" Mikey offered a huge grin. "'Bout time you decided to drop by. I thought you was knocking 'em dead on the rodeo circuit. What the hell you doin' back here in this shithole?"

"Ain't nothin' like a warm welcome, huh, Caleb?" The deep, sexy voice of Evelyn, Mikey's wife, washed over him like warm water.

Caleb nodded in the woman's direction. Perched on a bar stool, she was still slender, her age slowly catching up with her. But the small wrinkles bracketing her mouth and fine lines softening her eyes just added to her prettiness.

"Good to see you, Evelyn."

"Same here, cowboy." She uncrossed her long legs, clad in faded denim, and stepped over to the table, reaching out to rub his shoulder fondly. "You home for good?"

"Hell, I'm not sure." Caleb offered a smile he knew fell short. "Maybe." He gestured toward the swinging half-door beyond the liquor display. "DeeDee still around?"

"She retired to Florida, oh, maybe two years ago. We bought her out. She gave us a good deal, just asked us to leave the name as DeeDee's, which wasn't a problem for us." Evelyn grinned. "Crotchety old biddy. Then she gave us that fancy sign to hang outside and it was a done deal."

Caleb remembered DeeDee well. Mean, grouchy, and no-nonsense, with a face like a horse and as wide as she was tall. "Well, I hope she hooks up with some hardbody on the beach and gets herself a regular lube job." While Evelyn snorted with laughter, Caleb called over, "Hey, Mikey, where the hell's that beer?"

Mikey slid one over. "Sorry, buddy, here ya go."

Evelyn coughed out a final chuckle, then gave Caleb a steady stare, her eyebrows raised in question.

"What?" But Caleb had a feeling he knew what she wanted to ask.

"Nothing, honey. Glad you're back." With a final pat, this time to his unbruised cheek, she picked up an empty tray and headed toward the billiard room to collect dirty glasses.

"You want a burger plate?" Mikey asked.

"Yeah. Loaded." Caleb rested his booted foot on his thigh to ease the stiffness in his sore leg, and gulped half the bottle of beer.

Mikey shouted the order to the bearded cook working behind the kitchen window, then turned back to Caleb. He wiped the bar with a wet towel. "You seen Rosemary yet?"

Fuck. Does the whole town know?

"Yeah. I saw her."

"You seen her boy?"

"You mean *my* boy."

"The little guy sure looks like you."

"I noticed." Caleb finished off his beer and motioned for another one.

Just as Mikey set it down, his daughter Adrianne strode from the kitchen and slammed a plate in front of Caleb. "Nice of you to come back, you bastard."

Whoa. This was getting crazy. If things kept up, he'd be run out of town. Did they still tar and feather undesirables?

"Hi, Adrianne, good to see you, too." He flashed the smile that got him plenty of action on the circuit, and quite a bit here in town, too—back in the day.

"Don't try that crap on me, cowboy." Adrianne drew up a chair and sat, her elbow on the table, resting her chin on her palm. "You seen him yet?"

Before he could answer, she reached out and grasped his chin, turning his head one way, then the other. "From the look of that fading shiner, I'd say Mason got hold of you already."

"If you're finished prying into my personal business, I'd like to eat my dinner."

Adrianne shrugged and snapped her gum. "Sure. Have at it, cowboy." She stood and swiped his longneck. Tilting her head back, she downed it in one long, easy gulp. "Thanks for the beer." Holding the now empty bottle, she sauntered away.

Caleb stared after her, marveling at how fast the girl could drink down a full longneck, and then walk without staggering. "More and more like her mama, isn't she?" He glanced at Mikey, who nodded and puffed out his chest proudly.

"That she is. But smart with it. Ev and I never have to worry about Adrianne. She can hold her own."

"She'd have to in this cow town, wouldn't she?" Caleb muttered, digging into his food.

Well, so far his welcome home had pretty much sucked. He hadn't expected a brass band to meet him at the bus stop or the mayor to present him with the golden key to the city, but neither had he figured on getting punched out by his best friend.

And aside from all that, he was faced with a genuine problem. He had a son. Carson.

Fuck me twice.

If his calculations were correct, the kid was about five years old. Did he even know who his father was? Did Rosemary ever talk about him? And if she did, was it to let the boy know his daddy was a loser who ran out on his mother?

A heavy hand landed on his shoulder. "Hiya, Caleb."

Caleb turned to face Dave Jamison, former high school football star, and from the looks of it, current deputy sheriff. Great. Was a jail cell his next stop?

"Hey, Dave. How's it going?"

Dave grabbed a chair and straddled it. "Good. Real good." He rested his arms on the back of the chair, and gave him a steady look. "I heard you've been back a few days."

Caleb laid down his half-eaten burger. "Small towns. Lots of gossip. Folks around here need to get some hobbies. I can't figure why my coming back to the town I was raised in would be such a newsworthy event. Why don't y'all go chase the kids who scribbled on the school building?"

Dave broke into a grin. "Don't see why you're getting yourself all worked up. I just came by to say hello."

"I'm sorry." Caleb ran his palm down his face. "I'm still trying to catch up to myself."

"I understand. So, how's things on the rodeo circuit? I hear you've been winning medals left and right."

Caleb shrugged. "A few. But I'll be out of commission for a while." At Dave's raised eyebrows, he continued, "An ornery bull threw me and decided that wasn't enough, so he landed on my leg. Busted it up in a few places."

"Damn."

"Yeah. It's all fixed up now, but I need a couple more months before I can return to the circuit."

If I can ever return.

"Well, we're happy to see you again. Just keep your nose clean while you're here."

The deputy's chuckle grated on Caleb's nerves. But then he'd been out of sorts since he came face to face with his past. At least Dave wasn't punching his lights out or slamming food down in front of him.

"So, what's new with you?" Caleb eyed the uniform Dave wore. "I see you're one of Laramie County's finest. Been doing it long?"

"Yeah, right after you ran out of town to make a name for yourself. Went through the academy, and been wearing the blues since then. I like it. It suits me."

"Locking up all those kids who damage school buildings?"

"And keeping an eye on newcomers to town with busted up legs."

"Ha. Not a newcomer, Jamison, a returnee." He pushed away his empty plate and signaled for another beer. "Can I buy you a drink?"

"Nah. Thanks. I'm waiting for my girl." He shot Caleb a knowing look. "She's gonna meet me here for dinner." He took a vibrating iPhone out of his pocket and glanced at the screen. "And, she just pulled in."

Dave looked up as the door opened. "Hi, darlin'. Just saying hello to an old friend of yours."

Caleb took a swig of beer and turned to stare directly into Rosemary Carmichael's stormy amber eyes.

Chapter Four

Rosemary's stomach fluttered with awareness when she spotted Caleb sitting at the bar with Dave. The memory of their time together still burned bright in her mind. The pain of his desertion was just as fresh today as it'd been all those years ago.

Why couldn't he have just stayed away?

Caleb turned toward her with a hard stare. A fresh wave of anger rolled through her, instantly smothering her hurt and leaving only steam behind. He had no right to be angry with her. He was the jackass.

She was so over Caleb Johnson! Been there. Done that.

Didn't need the heartache again.

She snorted. Hell, her life was a damn country song. Squaring her shoulders, Rosemary marched inside and up to Dave, wrapping her arms around his waist and lifting her face for a kiss.

Dave grinned, his eyes gleaming with amusement, because their relationship so far was more friends than lovers, and he'd only kissed her once. He'd understand her brazen display was for Caleb's benefit. But being the gentleman he was, Dave didn't let her down. He threaded his fingers through her hair and leaned in, giving her a deep kiss.

But just like the other time he'd kissed her, she felt nothing. Not even a tiny sensual quiver. Zilch. Instead, Caleb's image floated behind her eyelids.

God! I'm in serious trouble.

She thought of Carson, her little angel, and was able to rein in her betraying emotions. There was no way she'd allow Caleb to crush her son's tender heart into the dirt on his way back out of town.

The sound of a heavy thud broke the kiss, and she glanced up to see Caleb glowering at them, beer foaming over his longneck bottle and running across his tightly gripped knuckles.

Her feeling of satisfaction was quickly followed by guilt. She'd never been the vindictive sort, and she shouldn't care whether Caleb was jealous or not. They had no future, only a sad history.

Caleb wasn't a keeper. He'd never stay. She needed to protect Carson from the same kind of heartache she'd suffered when she'd awoken alone, abandoned . . . pregnant. Every tender promise he'd made, a lie. All damn lies.

"So, Caleb," Dave asked, "how long are you in town for?" He tucked her close to his side.

"Don't know. Depends." Steel threaded his voice as he turned away from them. "Mikey, another Bud."

"Be right there," Mikey called over his shoulder as he served two fruity-looking concoctions to a couple of young women at the end of the bar.

"Well. Um," Rosemary stammered as the air sizzled with awkward, uncomfortable tension. "I guess we should get a table."

"I already have one picked out, darlin'."

With his arm still around her waist and a smirk on his lips, Dave steered her toward the dining area. He led her to a corner table and held out her chair so she could sit, then leaned down and nuzzled her neck, before taking a seat across from her.

She groaned under her breath when she saw she had a direct view of the bar, and Caleb. His brooding gaze rested on her as he picked up his beer and took a long draw. *Not. Good.* She'd known him most of her life, and his body posture indicated he was seriously pissed off.

Irritated, Rosemary turned her attention to Dave.

He stared back with a wide-eyed innocent expression. "What?"

"You were baiting him."

A grin split his face. "Yeah. Isn't that what you wanted?"

Was it?

She shook her head in silent denial. Caleb wasn't worth the emotion it'd take to rile him up. She'd already spent too many years crying over him. He meant nothing to her now.

That's not fair and you know it. She stifled a sigh. No, it wasn't fair.

There'd been times, before she and Caleb ever hooked up, that he'd listened to her woes and offered a shoulder, advice; hell, just an open ear. When her mama was driving her nuts or her daddy got itchy and they all wondered if he'd make it through another weekend without bolting. She'd vent and Caleb would display a lot of patience for a guy willingly dealing with an idiot teenage girl.

She shook herself from the memories when Adrianne stopped by and took their orders. Neither she nor Dave needed a menu;

Rosemary had eaten here often enough to know exactly what she wanted. She shot a quick glance toward Caleb, noting the two women from the end of the bar had sidled up next to him. Her mouth tightened, the momentary softening she'd felt toward him fading fast.

He seemed quite content to have those bimbos fawn over him. Something ugly rose up inside her and for a second or two she wanted to rush over and pull out their bottle-blonde hair. Rosemary forced her attention back to Dave, who was watching her now with solemn, knowing eyes.

To his credit, he didn't say anything.

Now it was her turn to ask, "What?"

Dave leaned over the small table and took her hand. "Rosemary, you and Carson mean a lot to me."

Rosemary shifted uncomfortably, reluctant to have this discussion. There'd never be anything more than friendship between them. She thought he understood.

Her brows squeezed together. Damn it. She just wanted to enjoy Dave's company, eat dinner, see a movie . . . and forget Caleb Johnson ever existed.

Dave chuckled, although the sound was devoid of humor. Still holding her fingers loosely, he brought his other hand up and tucked a wayward strand of hair behind her ear. "Relax, darlin'. I know you don't feel the same way. I get that."

Rosemary smiled sadly, not knowing what to say. She didn't deserve his friendship. "I'm sorry, Dave. You're a great guy—"

"Whoa!" He released her hand and sat back in his chair, bringing both his palms up in a 'stop' gesture. "Don't give me the 'you're a great guy, we can be friends' line." The look he gave her held real affection this time. "I know you and Caleb have a history. Hell, everyone knows Carson's his."

She didn't deny it—never had—although she didn't talk about it either. "Ancient history. There's nothing between us now."

The words rolled off her tongue easily enough, and yet they tasted like a lie. She frowned, picking up her dinner napkin and spreading it across her lap.

He clucked his tongue. "That's not exactly true, darlin'. There's Carson. And regardless of how things work out between us, I want you both to be happy."

Her emotions churning, a tear slid down her cheek. Why couldn't she have fallen for someone like Dave? He was handsome, solid, and dependable. Not some footloose cowboy with dreams of being a rodeo star. Even six years ago she knew Caleb could easily end up breaking her heart. "Carson and I are happy."

He brought his thumb to her cheek and swiped at her tears. "Are you? From what I can see, you're so tied up in Caleb you can't move on, can't give another guy a chance."

"That's not true. I've dated plenty," she denied, though she knew he was speaking the truth.

Evelyn dropped off their drinks with a quick smile for them both, and Rosemary reached for her margarita. She needed something to help her relax. Her nerves were strung tight.

Dave lifted his frosty beer mug, his expression pure devilment. "Maybe you need some help working him out of your system."

She choked on her drink, giving him an incredulous look. He was so full of it. Damn, but he was cute, with that golden brown buzz cut and those twinkling hazel eyes. Why couldn't she have fallen for him, instead of the town heartbreaker? Still, her tension eased and she laughed. "Are you offering, cowboy?"

He grinned at her over the top of his mug, and took a swig, then wiped the foam from his mouth with the back of his hand before replying, "Maybe."

Setting his mug down, his expression grew serious. "Or maybe you need to give him another shot, or at least an opportunity to know his son. Then you'll be able to finally move on."

Should he have the right to know his son? No! He abandoned us.

But he hadn't known about Carson. He'd only abandoned *her.*

Rosemary looked back at the bar and her stomach clenched, hurt rushing through her veins. Caleb had his arm around a floozie's waist as she stared up at him like some puppy dog looking for a bone.

But his glittering gaze was solidly locked on Rosemary, even as the woman's hand crawled up his chest. Then the other bimbo leaned over and whispered something in his ear as she pressed up against his back. He glanced around to the voluptuous blonde, and smiled.

A smile he used to turn on her right before he made love to her.

A smile he now gave to two sluts in a bar; one he'd probably been giving to women all across the rodeo circuit, along with his body.

Rosemary's heart hardened and she turned away as Adrianne came up to their table with their meals. No, she didn't want Caleb Johnson.

But did that give her the right to keep him away from his son?

Chapter Five

Right about the same time Rosemary finished her meal and got to her feet, Caleb realized the last thing he wanted was a couple of local barflies hanging all over him. The hurt look she cast him, before glancing quickly away, made him feel like a real jerk.

Busy detaching the blonde's inch-long fingernails from his shirtsleeve, he glanced toward the dining room again, just in time to see Rosemary pause next to Dave, slip her purse strap over her shoulder, then lean in and kiss the bastard's cheek. Dave watched the sway of her jeans-clad hips all the way to the door.

Caleb wanted to rip off Dave's head and stuff it up his ass. And then confront Rosemary. Remove the pain from where it burned a hole in his gut as if he'd eaten acid. Clear the air between them, once and for all.

He'd purposely stayed away from her for two days, reacquainting himself with the slower pace of Dustin, trying to take it easy on his leg. He'd looked up a few old, still-local friends, even reconnected with his Uncle Zip, spending an hour or so the other night yakking to him long distance to Rock Springs, where Zip had landed after leaving Dustin. Most of his meals Caleb had eaten at the diner off Main.

Some needed space. That had been his aim. For Rosemary, and for him.

Pointless.

Easing off the barstool, he fished in his pocket for a twenty, tossing it on the counter. Over the drunken protests of the women he'd pushed away, Caleb took the side 'Bar Only' entrance and slipped out. In those damned sexy high-heeled boots, Rosemary wouldn't have gotten halfway across the parking lot yet.

Sure enough, he spotted her a short distance away, near the floodlight over DeeDee's fancy new sign. Rosemary's head was bent and all that gorgeous red hair sheltered her face from his view. She dug through her purse, probably searching for her keys.

Aside from the need for confrontation, he worried to think she'd walk around Dustin with her head down after evening set in. Not paying attention to anyone who could just step up and grab her arm.

Yeah, like me. His mouth set into a grim line at her careless regard for her own safety.

Not breaking his stride, Caleb reached her in under five seconds, taking her arm in a firm grip. With a feminine squeak of protest, she spun toward him.

He caught a brief flash of her lacy black bra as the deep vee of her sleeveless blouse gapped revealingly. For a second he had a chance to admire the way her skin looked like cream against the lace.

With an irritated huff, she started squirming and pulling at his hand. "Damn it, let go, Caleb. What the hell do you think you're doing?"

"We gotta talk." Wanting some privacy from nosy townsfolks, he maneuvered her away from the floodlight and off the sidewalk, stopping just inside the alley where empty boxes had been stacked for trash pickup.

She tugged harder. "Nothing to talk about. Let go."

"Nope." He'd sucked down enough beer to take the sensible edge off his brain. "I've got some things to say to you." He backed her into the nearest brick wall and slapped his hands on her shoulders to prevent her from bolting. "You're damned well gonna listen."

Rosemary shoved her hair out of her face and gave him one hell of a stink eye. "You're drunk and an asswipe. Want to talk about that?" Under his palms, the set of her shoulders tightened like a cocked bow.

"I want to know what Jamison is to you," Caleb growled.

She stiffened even more. "None of your business. Now get your hands off me!"

Releasing her shoulders, he slammed his palms onto the wall behind her, not touching her, but still blocking her exit. "Better?" he growled.

She stared up at him silently. In the dim alley lighting he could see how anger lit her up, more than likely making her too furious to speak. Well, tough, because they had a thing or two to get straight.

"And it *is* my damned business, Rosie. The man's a skirt chaser and if he's hanging around my son—"

Caleb got no further because Rosemary was suddenly in his face, one slender finger drilling into his chest. "You don't get to say who hangs out with *my* son. You sure as hell don't get a vote in who chases my frigging skirt."

She poked his chest harder. "You don't know a thing about me, or Dave, or what's gone on in this town since you've been goddamned gone."

"Knock it off." Beyond irritated, he grabbed for her hand, yanking her closer. Until every inch of the denim and cotton she wore was plastered against him. Her breath hitched, and the rapid rise and fall of her breasts made Caleb break out in a sudden sweat.

The jealousy and anger roaring through him switched off like a light bulb. All he could concentrate on was Rosemary.

God, he could smell her, some kind of flowery stuff he remembered she always used on her hair. Her lips parted and he caught a tang of the margaritas she'd had. The feel of her body brought back memories of hot nights, damp bedsheets twisted on the floor, long, tangled curls; fingernails digging into his bare shoulders.

He stared down into her beautiful face. She'd been a pretty kid, an adorable teenager. And almost too much woman for him at nineteen, in spite of her innocence. Now she simply knocked him sideways. He wanted her. Hell, he'd never stopped wanting her.

The thought of her dating a guy Caleb used to consider a friend . . . *Damn it all to hell.*

He couldn't take it.

Dave Jamison, kissing her, his fingers twined into those gorgeous, fiery locks. Holding her with arms that didn't belong around her tiny waist, mere inches from the breasts Caleb had been the first to claim. She'd smiled at Dave. *And frowned at me.*

The ten-second kissing scene he'd been forced to watch in DeeDee's bar played over and over in Caleb's brain until he groaned aloud. The flash of desire he'd managed to bank suddenly came back with ferocity. Asswipe that he was, he let it take him over.

Grasping her by the arms, Caleb pressed her back into the wall again, then lowered his face until his lips were an inch from hers. He registered the shock in her eyes, dilating the amber until they were almost black.

"Caleb—" She swallowed and licked her lips. The hint of protest in her voice when she uttered his name should have resulted with him treading softly. But then her fingers curled into his shirt lapels and she tugged. Hard. Toward her.

Against her.

Jesus.

On a groan, he took her mouth hungrily. Her taste exploded on his tongue as he dove deep.

Deeper.

He raked a hand over her blouse, finding an opening between buttons, slipping his fingers inside on a search for silky flesh. The lacy bra she wore barely covered her, and he cupped a firm breast. Six years simply disintegrated into nothing as he relearned her skin, the way she trembled in his arms, how her tongue met his with aggression. Rosie Carmichael had never been a shrinking violet at nineteen, and she wasn't one now.

Closer, damn it. Caleb didn't realize he'd spoken aloud until she moaned a high, thin, "God, yes," into his mouth and opened her stance, rocking on her high heeled boots. He thrust his free hand under her bottom and hoisted her up so she could wrap a leg around his hips, a sensual anchor. Now her fingers were buried in his hair, gripping it tightly enough to rip out chunks. The pain only added fuel to his overloaded system. He pinned her harder against the old brick wall.

Tearing his lips from hers, he ran them down the side of her slender throat, nipping the hot skin, lingering at the curve of shoulder and neck where he knew she was most sensitive. When he bit down, a shudder passed through her body. She untangled the fingers of one hand from his hair and scraped her nails over his chest, to the edge of his jeans, until she reached his button fly. Her palm caged him there, one eager press against the denim covering his hard-on.

"Christ," he muttered, moving his hips in time with her strokes. He raised his head until he could engulf her mouth in another exploring kiss. Her breath hitched and the tiny sob she loosed against his tongue belied the way she clutched him tighter. "Rosie . . ."

"Rosie, what the hell!"

The words, uttered in an angry male voice, came from behind them and she froze in his arms, pulling her lips from his, uncurling her fingers from his scalp. She snatched her hand from his groin and dropped her face to his shoulder. Through his shirt he could feel the heat of embarrassment that emanated from her cheeks.

Caleb glanced behind him and cursed under his breath as Mason stomped over.

"Get away from her, Johnson," he snarled.

"I'm not holding on." Caleb relaxed his arms and let them hang at his sides. The only connection remaining was Rosemary's leg curled around his hips. Her face was still buried in his neck. "Your sister's where she wants to be. Take a hike, Carmichael, before I forget we're friends."

"We're not friends, you son of a bitch. Not any longer." Mason stepped closer and sent his sister a scathing glare. "Rosie, Carson's running a fever. Susan called me when she couldn't get hold of you. I tried calling too, but your phone must be dead."

"Oh, Lord." She slapped her hands on Caleb's chest and pushed him away. "I forgot to charge it! I'm sorry. How high of a fever? I'm sorry—"

She stepped around him and plucked her purse off the ground where it had fallen when he'd held her against the wall.

In that moment, with all of her attention on their son, Caleb knew whatever bond they'd begun forming had cracked. Like hell he'd let go of that bit of reconnection. He swung to face Mason's ire and stated calmly, "I'll go with you."

"No fucking way," Mason bit out, surging toward him.

Rosemary dug her fingers into her brother's arm and held him back. "I can handle this, Mason. Caleb has a right to see his son—"

"Why, because he shoved his tongue down your throat and felt you up in a damned alley? You think that means you're better than any other piece of ass he's planked from here to Casper?"

Caleb had heard enough. "Goddamn it, watch your mouth." He eased Rosemary aside and shot out a hand, fisting Mason's shirt collar and dragging him to his toes, uncaring that he was choking him. If Mason wanted to throw down with him again, he'd oblige.

"Caleb, let him go." Rosemary tugged at his hand.

Caleb tightened his fingers, wringing a grunt from Mason, before abruptly releasing him. Mason stumbled but managed to stay upright. Fury and something else that Caleb hoped might be shame radiated from him.

"Call me anything you like, but never speak to your sister that way again, you got me?" Caleb stared him down, until Mason looked away, muttering under his breath.

Reaching for her hand, Caleb pulled her toward the parking lot. "Let's go." He didn't wait for her acquiescence, but strode to where several cars were parked. "Which one's yours?"

"The blue Honda." She pointed to a little Civic. Now she was the one pulling him. "Hurry, okay? Fevers really scare me."

"We'll take care of him, honey. He'll be all right," Caleb assured her.

As he climbed into the passenger seat and Rosemary gunned the engine, Caleb hoped to hell he wasn't lying.

Chapter Six

Rosemary peeled out of the parking lot like a seasoned Indy 500 driver, which only increased the knots in Caleb's stomach. Little kids got fevers all the time, right? Following on the heels of that thought was how many years Rosemary had done this all on her own while he'd been out there making a name for himself. The only name that applied now was *asshole*.

They tore through town before turning onto Smithy Road, which led to an older section of Dustin. Screeching down Benson Drive, she barely brought the car to a complete stop before she flung her door open and raced toward the front porch of a small, older two-story house.

Caleb steeled himself to meet his kid for real this time. He grabbed the keys she'd left in the ignition and followed Rosemary up the porch stairs and into the house. Despite his worry, he took note of the place where she and her son—no, *their* son—lived. The interior of the house was as tidy as the outside. From what he could sense, Rosemary's presence was in every corner of the cozy rooms.

Is this what our home would have looked like if I'd stuck around long enough to find out I was going to be a father?

There was no doubt in his mind he would have married Rosemary. Even if Mason hadn't been standing behind him with a shotgun. But a little voice in the back of his head told him he'd have grown to resent her. Back in the day, his only focus was the rodeo, and how big a name he could make for himself. Looking back now at his wins and losses, and his resultant injury, it all seemed so childish.

Rosemary's boots beat a cadence as she hurried up the carpeted stairs, then made an abrupt turn into an open bedroom door. Without waiting for an invitation he followed her.

The wail of a crying child and a woman's low, soothing voice greeted him. Carson slumped on the bed, bent over, and from where Caleb stood the kid's breathing was not sounding good. Rosemary sat alongside the boy and touched his forehead. She gasped and looked at Susan, pacing near the window. "He's so hot."

"I gave him some children's fever reducer a little while ago, but it didn't seem to work," Susan stopped pacing and shot Caleb a don't-mess-with-my-best-friend glare. "And his breathing is pretty bad."

Caleb felt like a third wheel here. Rosemary and Susan had probably been through something like this before. Totally clueless on how things worked with kids, fevers, and breathing problems, all he could think of was how they needed to get him to an emergency room. Carson's lips were blue as he struggled to take in air. The worry Caleb felt kicked any residual buzz from his brain, instantly alert as he studied his son's flushed cheeks.

After years of watching medical emergencies from stomped-on cowboys along the circuit, his normal decisive attitude took over. He strode to the bed, scooped Carson up, blankets and all, and headed for the door. "Hang on, buddy," he said, as the boy laid his head on his chest.

"What the hell do you think you're doing?" Rosemary yelled as she ran after him. "Put my son down."

Pausing, he said quietly, "I'm taking *our* son to the emergency room."

Susan flanked his other side, tugging on Caleb's arm. "You have no right."

"Get out of my way. I have every right." He nudged Susan aside and cast a glance over his shoulder to a stunned Rosemary. "Let's go."

Either his growl or her motherly instinct kicked in because she quickly grabbed a furry stuffed animal from the boy's bed, and raced behind him.

"Rosemary, you can't let him do this," Susan shouted from the top of the stairs as Caleb shifted Carson to open the front door.

"He's right, Susan. Carson needs help." Rosemary followed him out into the dark night.

She climbed into the passenger seat and held her arms out to Caleb. He placed Carson on her lap and strode to the other side. "Is the hospital still on Baker and Montrose?"

"Yeah." Her voice had gone thick with emotion.

Caleb glanced briefly at Carson. "Has he had breathing problems before?"

"Not like this. Only the usual colds and some allergies, but this is bad. He started coughing yesterday morning but I thought it was just a summer cold." Rosemary chewed her plump lips, where only about ten minutes ago he'd been happily nibbling. He shook his head to clear it from those thoughts. Right now they had to get Carson taken care of.

Caleb reached out and touched her hand. "It will be all right. The doctors will fix him right up."

Why did his assurance calm her down? Caleb knew nothing about children, fevers, or anything else that she'd lived with—alone—all these years. But seeing his determined face as he whipped around cars on their race to the hospital did just that. It had always been Mason who'd stepped in to take on the role of daddy when she'd needed him to. Now she had to deal with Carson's actual father. But for how long?

She hugged her son's overly-warm body closer and looked out the window at the stores and houses as they whizzed by. It was best not to get used to Caleb being here. Sure, he was taking charge now, and acted the part of the doting father, but her heart told her he'd up and leave as soon as whatever it was that brought him back here was fixed.

She hadn't missed his slight limp and occasional wince when he moved. He'd obviously decided to take a little time off to recover from an injury. But why here? His parents had left town years ago. *Did he choose Dustin because of me?* She snorted. Even she wasn't stupid enough to believe that.

The car came to a screeching halt outside Emergency. She'd managed to unfasten her seatbelt about a second before Caleb wrenched her door open. He gently took Carson from her arms, then rushed toward the entrance, leaving her gaping after them.

"Wait!" She scrambled to catch up as they all reached the reception desk.

"What have we here?" The night duty nurse looked over the top of her computer monitor as the emergency doors slid closed with a whoosh.

"My son has a high fever and he's having a lot of trouble breathing," Rosemary said.

"All right. Follow me and we'll get him checked out." The nurse led them to an empty bed and pulled up the safety rails. "Please lay him down there," she instructed Caleb.

"Mommy." Carson stretched out his hand. Rosemary placed her palm on his forehead, *Still so hot*. She looked down at his frightened little face and her stomach did a whirl.

"Sir, if you'll come with me, you can give me the boy's insurance information and whatever else we need."

"Rosie," Caleb said, "maybe you should do that."

"No. I'm staying here with Carson." She gripped his little fingers as if to anchor herself from being dragged from the room.

He sighed. "I don't know the information she's going to ask."

"Ma'am." The nurse regarded her with sympathy. "Let his daddy stay with him. It'll only take a few minutes to get the paperwork filled out."

His daddy. Had Carson heard her? She glanced down at her son, who was having trouble taking a breath. *God, I hope not.*

Rosemary had to beat down the desire to lash out at the nurse as she followed her to the reception desk. She and Carson had always done just fine on their own. Fighting off tears, she fished around in her purse for her insurance card. Carson belonged to only her. How could she share him now?

"The little guy sure looks like his daddy."

Gritting her teeth, Rosemary handed the card over. The low-pitched tones of Caleb's soothing voice carried into the hallway. What was he saying to her son?

After signing numerous forms she returned to Carson's bedside just as another nurse entered. "We have a little bit of a breathing problem, young man?" The middle-aged woman smiled at Carson as she took his pulse, then swiped his forehead with a thermometer. She moved to the computer and entered information. The night nurse came back into the room with a plastic bracelet that she fastened to Carson's wrist.

"How bad is his temperature?" Rosemary tried to look over the attending nurse's shoulder at the computer screen, but couldn't see the numbers.

"It's slightly over one hundred and two."

Fear gripped her stomach. "That's dangerous, isn't it?"

The nurse approached the side of Carson's bed and put a blood pressure cuff on him. "Children tend to have higher fevers than adults. It's not unusual."

All this time Caleb had been hovering on the other side of Carson's bed, his face creased with worry. Now he moved to stand beside her, slipping his arm around her shoulders. She allowed herself to relax into his strength, the warmth of his body easing her chills, before remembering where she was at and who she was with.

She glanced sideways at Caleb. "You don't have to stay. Though I do appreciate the help."

A stubborn expression formed on his handsome face. "Aside from the fact I have no car, I plan to stay right here until I know what our boy's problem is."

Rosemary fought to keep her cool. Lord, the man had her twisted in knots and he'd only been back in town for a couple of days.

"Mommy, my chest hurts."

She slid out from under Caleb's arm and stepped to the bed to sit alongside her son. "I know, sweetheart. That's why we're here. The doctor will come in and make you feel all better."

This was certainly not the time or place to resurrect the feelings of abandonment she'd suffered when the doctor confirmed her pregnancy and she had no idea where Caleb was.

Carson nodded as another bout of coughing overtook him. His face turned red and he gagged for a minute before leaning back against the pillow, looking so small and vulnerable in the baggy hospital gown.

"Where the hell is the doctor?" Caleb growled, and began to pace around the bed.

Rosemary pushed the hair back from Carson's forehead, her heart speeding up when she felt the heat coming from his body. Yes, where the hell was the doctor?

After about ten minutes of Carson coughing, Caleb pacing, and Rosemary ready to pull her hair out, the doctor knocked softly on the door and pushed it open.

"Good evening." He stuck his hand out to Caleb. "I'm Dr. Vine." He nodded in Rosemary's direction. "I understand we have a sick little boy here."

"He started coming down with a cold a couple of days ago, but tonight his coughing got much worse and he has a pretty high fever." Rosemary pushed aside her anxiety and strove to respond as calmly as possible.

"Well, let's take a listen." The doctor moved to Carson's side and placed a stethoscope against his chest. From the wince he made, the instrument must have been cold. Dr. Vine frowned and moved the stethoscope to Carson's back.

"Pneumonia," he pronounced, after a few more checks.

"Pneumonia!" She and Caleb said at the same time.

"Yes, sir. This little guy has pneumonia."

Rosemary burst into tears. What kind of a mother was she that her son developed pneumonia and she thought it was only a cold?

Carson coughed, his small body jerking from the strain. Caleb moved to her side and once again slipped his arms around her. "It'll be all right."

"Now, now, mother. These things happen. Kids can go from being fine to very sick in no time. Remember, when we adults are sick, we start to think about taking care of the problem right away. A child usually ignores any symptoms until he's flat on his back."

"So what needs to be done?" Caleb asked, worry evident in his voice.

"Given his fever and his age, I'm going to admit him."

Helpless fear made her tremble. *I hate falling apart like this.* Especially in front of Caleb. She'd handled all of Carson's illnesses and other mishaps on her own, no problem. Now she was acting like a sobbing teenager in a bad movie.

She pulled away and wiped her cheeks. "I want to spend the night here with him."

"That should be no problem. I'll have him transferred to Pediatrics and you can work that out with the nurses."

The doctor looked briefly at Caleb before he turned to the computer and began typing furiously. "It might be a problem if you both want to stay."

"It'll just be me," Rosemary replied.

Dr. Vine merely gave a quick nod and continued entering information. Rosemary raised her chin and regarded Caleb. "I'm going to run home and pick up a few things. I can drop you off wherever you're staying."

Caleb tensed. Rosemary waited for him to disagree with her, but then he gave a curt nod. "All right. I'm at the Bronco Inn. Unit Fourteen."

"That studio Nash rents by the week?"

"Yeah."

"That's a decent room." Feeling more in control of herself now, she sat on the edge of the bed and stroked Carson's cheek. "Mommy's going home to get a few things so I can stay overnight with you."

"Don't leave." Two tears tracked down his sweet face as he gripped her hand.

"I won't be gone long, promise." She leaned in and kissed his forehead.

"No." Carson peeked at Caleb from under lowered lashes. "Can't the man go and get your things?"

"He doesn't know what to get, or where to find things, honey. Suppose I call Aunt Susie to bring what I need?"

After another lengthy bout of coughing, Carson nodded and collapsed against the pillow.

"I'm going to have the nurse give him a breathing treatment before he goes upstairs." Apparently having finished what he needed to do on the computer, Dr. Vine opened the door and was gone in a flash.

"I don't like that doctor." Caleb frowned at the door as it swung shut. "He spent more time on the computer than he did looking at Carson."

"I have to agree with you there." She pulled her phone from her pocket. "Carson, I'm going to step outside and call Aunt Susie to bring my things. But I'll be right back, and I'll only be on the other side of the door, okay?"

She elbowed Caleb. "Would you mind joining me?"

He blinked, but nodded. "Sure."

Once they were far enough away from the door that Carson wouldn't be able to hear them, she came to an abrupt halt and turned. "What did you say to Carson while I was at the reception desk?"

Caleb arched a questioning brow. "Nothing. Just tried to keep him entertained."

"Good . . . good." There was a beat of silence. "If I decide to tell Carson you're his father, it'll be when I feel the time is right."

He rubbed the back of his neck and sighed. "I get that, Rosie."

"Excuse me?" A young candy striper wheeled up a cart with a pitcher of juice and some glasses. "Would you like something to drink?"

Glad for the interruption, Rosemary stepped away from him. "We'll talk about this later."

Chapter Seven

Caleb paced the waiting room of the hospital, where he'd spent most of the past several days wearing a path in the carpeting as he worried about his son.

My son!

His hand clenched at his side, still unable to wrap those words around his brain. The anxiety flooding his body was a new emotion for him. The fear ran so deep, it squeezed the oxygen from his lungs. And he'd left Rosie to deal with this by herself over the last five years.

Which made him a first-class dirtbag, and he wasn't sure how to make it up to her. He'd do everything in his power to gain her forgiveness, because he was determined to be there for Carson from here on out.

"Mr. Johnson," the young, friendly nurse said as she approached him. "Ms. Carmichael would like you to join her in Carson's room."

His heart pounded hard as he rushed down the hall. *Is something wrong?*

Although still upset with him, at least Rosemary hadn't shut him out, allowing him to spend time each day with Carson. Even sick and feverish, his son was sweet and funny, and now owned a huge chunk of Caleb's heart. There wasn't anything he wouldn't do for that little boy.

When he entered the room, Rosemary and the doctor stood next to Carson's bed.

"Caleb." Her face glowed. "Carson's being released today."

The gut-deep relief he felt at that news made the wandering-cowboy part of him cry 'uncle' as a protective instinct he didn't know he had slammed into him. A fist squeezed inside his chest as he watched Rosemary feather slender fingers through Carson's hair, before leaning in to tenderly kiss his rosy cheek, murmuring, "Mommy loves you, little man."

She was an amazing mother, and had done a wonderful job raising their boy. But from here on out, Carson would get the benefit of both his parents.

Caleb closed the distance between him and his son to peer down at him. He winked. "Hey, champ. Ready to get out of here?"

He nodded, smiling shyly, then asked, "Are you my daddy?"

A barely audible gasp fell from Rosemary's lips.

Dr. Vine cleared his throat and headed for the door at a quick pace. "I'll get that paperwork going for you."

Caleb's gaze shot to Rosemary as his heart pounded a staccato beat in his chest. "Thanks, Doc." He nervously rubbed his leg, somewhat sore from all his pacing. He truly did not want to screw this up.

Her hand pressing against her throat, she chewed on her plump bottom lip as she brought her attention to their son. "Carson—"

Caleb laid his hand on Rosemary's shoulder and gave it a soft squeeze. "Rosie," he said quietly, "let me."

She glanced up at him, then back at Carson. "All right," she agreed hesitantly.

He advanced to the side of the bed, then ruffled Carson's hair, grinning in an attempt to keep it light. "Would that be okay with you, buddy?"

His breath hitched as he waited for his son's answer, not knowing what he'd do if Carson hated the idea. And it'd be Caleb's own damn fault for not being there for his boy.

A huge smile split Carson's cute cherub face. "That's great. Can I call you Daddy? Will you play baseball with me and Uncle Mason? Can we go get pizza? I like pizza!"

Caleb sighed in relief. Taking note of Rosemary's emotional state, giving her a moment to collect herself, he stroked his son's silky head. "You bet you can call me Daddy. And pizza's my favorite, too."

Rosemary laughed. "I'm sure Uncle Mason will love having your daddy play baseball with you."

The teasing tone in her voice was directed at him, and Caleb grinned at her as he felt the shift in their relationship. Although he didn't figure he was completely forgiven, at least Rosie seemed willing to give him a chance with their son. That was a good starting point and a much better place than when he'd first stepped off the bus, days ago.

Now Mason was a different story, and he really wasn't looking forward to that conversation. The few times he'd run into him at the hospital while visiting Carson hadn't been pretty. Caleb knew his old buddy would rather kick his ass than share Carson in a game of baseball. But for the boy's sake, Mason would have to come to grips with the fact that Caleb was here and wasn't leaving any time soon.

If ever.

Rosemary watched Carson and Caleb playing with matchbox cars on the floor of her living room. Seeing the two of them together, looking so much alike warmed her heart even as worry and hope warred inside her.

The past week had been a whirlwind of happenings, and she was emotionally exhausted. After another couple days of bedrest, Carson was almost back to normal. Caleb had brought over the pizza he'd promised, and she had the table all set.

Carson giggled as he ran his car across Caleb's broad chest. "Vroom. Vroom."

The deep rumble of Caleb's answering chuckle, as he rolled onto his back and lifted Carson above his head, slid across her body like a caress. Her center quivered as memories of their passionate embrace in DeeDee's alley filled her mind. If not for her brother showing up the other night, she would have let Caleb take her right there, up against the brick wall.

She shoved the memory aside. "Okay, you two. Come eat."

When she'd informed her brother that Carson knew about, and accepted Caleb as his father, he hadn't been pleased. For his nephew's sake, though, he'd deal. But Mason was a long way from forgiving Caleb for deserting her. As was Susan, who'd told her she'd be a fool to let that 'dirty, rotten cowboy' back into her life. Not that she could blame them, since she hadn't fully forgiven him herself.

Which made the way her body cried out for his touch—every time he was near, damn it—totally pathetic.

Caleb glanced at her from under thick lashes as Carson bounced on his eight-pack abs. His sexy grin and sinfully dark green eyes took her breath away as butterflies swarmed in her belly. She pressed her lips together, ignoring the tingling sensation between her legs, and silently told herself to knock it the hell off. That road would only lead to more heartache. She'd had little choice but to let Caleb into Carson's life, but no way was he getting back into her panties.

"You heard your mama, champ. Let's eat." He tossed Carson into the air one last time, before rolling to his feet and bringing Carson with him.

Her son clung to Caleb's hand, a look of hero-worship on his adorable face. "Pizza!" he yelled, rocking on his feet in excitement.

Rosemary could only stare, with her heart in her throat. Except for the bright red hair, Carson was the spitting image of his father. A tickle of unease rolled through her, worry that her baby's heart would be crushed when Caleb went back on the circuit. That thought hit like a bucket of cold water, bringing her back to her senses, and she frowned.

Studying her, Caleb arched one curious brow. "Everything okay?"

"Fine," she lied, turning and heading into the kitchen. They took their seats around the table, their pizza already cut and waiting, along with breadsticks and a pitcher of ice tea. Carson sat between them, his face beaming with happiness as he munched his slice of pizza.

"I'd like to stop over tomorrow and pick up Carson for the day, if that's all right," Caleb said, dipping a breadstick into the container of marinara sauce.

"I—I don't know," she said, concerned at the way her son lit up at Caleb's request. He was growing way too attached.

"Please, Mommy," Carson pleaded. His face had flushed with excitement.

As if to shut down her refusal, Caleb reached across the table and placed his hand over hers, giving it a light caress. Electricity zinged between them, and Rosemary felt it deep. Her resolve weakened.

"I thought maybe I'd take him to the park over near Hawthorn. I'd love it if you'd come along." His low voice coaxed and seduced. Against her better judgment she found herself agreeing. *Damn it.* She'd never been able to resist Caleb when he laid on the charm.

Turning to her son, Rosemary brushed his bangs off his forehead, leaning in to kiss the spot she'd bared. "Okay, sweetheart. But it's straight to bed tonight, with no squabbles. Agreed?"

He vigorously bobbed his head, wearing an ear-to-ear grin that was just like his father's. And she seemed helpless against both.

After the rest of their meal and yet another viewing of *Finding Nemo*, Carson jumped off Caleb's lap, where he'd sat the entire movie, and gave him a big hug. "'Night, Daddy."

"'Night, champ." Caleb's voice sounded suspiciously husky, his expression tender as he cupped his son's face.

For the first time, instead of only thinking of how his return to town affected her and Carson, she thought about Caleb.

She'd had a crush on him since she was twelve and he'd sauntered through her front door with her brother after a victorious football game. But Caleb had never seen her as anything more than Mason's little sister. Until six years ago when he'd rolled back into town, finally taking notice of her as a woman. She'd all but offered herself up to him on a silver platter.

Even though her heart was broken when he'd left without a word, she knew he *was* a good man. They'd both been young, and their one-week affair had been intense, but still . . . it'd only been a week.

So could she really blame him for following his dreams? Maybe it was time to release her anger so he could have a real relationship with his son.

While Rosemary settled Carson in bed, Caleb thought about what a great kid they'd created together. Their son was a joy to be around, sweet and well behaved but rambunctious enough to keep things interesting. Returning to the rodeo circuit suddenly didn't appeal to him as it had a few weeks ago. This time, unlike six years earlier, the idea of a more settled life didn't send him running for the hills.

And Rosie! Damn. She'd been a teasing temptation at nineteen, with flirty ways and a sassy attitude, but she'd grown into a mature, sexy-as-hell woman who took no shit and knew what she wanted. Given the way her eyes darkened whenever she looked his way . . . she wanted him.

He remembered her as a teenager, how sweet she'd been. Her sense of humor and the silly things she'd say, just to get a laugh from him. He also recalled a few times when he could talk to her, really open up about his dreams of making it big in the rodeo, and she'd listen. Caleb knew her folks fought like a couple of cats tied up in a bag, and Rosie had always been a sensitive kid. Too sensitive to have to deal with that shit, day after day. But she'd gotten past it. He was so proud of her.

And he sure as hell wanted her. Not just for a week, but for something like eternity.

Rising to his feet, he strode down the hall and stood outside Carson's room, listening to her tender words and Carson's sleepy giggles as she tucked him in for the night. The emotions he'd been drowning in over the last week fell away, replaced by an overwhelming need for Rosie. He wanted to make love to her, find a way to bring their relationship back where it'd been before he'd run off. He wanted to drown in their shared memories, then create new ones with her.

He absently rubbed his sore leg. He wasn't stupid; returning to the rodeo circuit was iffy for him. Maybe it was time to make a life for himself in Dustin, with Rosie and his son.

If she'd have him.

Her footsteps made a soft shuffle from the bedroom into the hall. Her breath hitched on a low gasp when she spotted him, then she slowly shut the door. "Hi," she murmured. "Is something the matter?"

Caleb closed the distance between them. He inhaled her heady fragrance, the same flowery perfume she'd worn six years ago when he'd explored every inch of her beautiful body, listening to the needy sounds she made as he'd discovered all her pleasure spots.

Oh, hell yeah. His muscles tight, he reached for her and ran one finger down the silken skin of her cheek as her lips parted on a sigh. Yet the resistance he read in her body language made his jaw clench.

"Caleb," she whispered, shaking her head. "We—we shouldn't."

Knowing he'd been her first lover filled him with such a sense of possessiveness. Though it was his own damned fault he'd lost her, he wanted to wipe away the imprint of any man who'd touched her over the last six years. To have her under him again, show her all the ways that she belonged to him, only him . . .

Gripping her gently by her upper arms, he leaned in and nuzzled her slender neck, flicking his tongue at the rapid pulse above her breasts. *Pleasure spot one.* At the sound of her sharp inhale, he nipped gently on her shoulder and tugged her closer. "Rosie." Her name was a shudder on his lips.

When he ran his tongue along the seam of her mouth she opened for him, allowing him to plunder her moist depths until she relaxed against him. Her arms slid around his neck as that sweet whimper he hadn't heard in six years sounded in her throat.

Victory coursed through him.

Chapter Eight

Bending slightly, Caleb slid one arm under Rosemary's knees and scooped her up. Her room was just down the hall and he strode the short distance quickly, kicking the door shut behind him. Lowering her to the bed, he followed her down, removing her arms from his neck and securing them above her head with one hand as he explored her curves.

Caleb's desire skyrocketed. He bent his head and pressed his mouth to hers, an open, urgent kiss, their tongues entwining in rising passion.

His fingers trembled as he went to work on the buttons of her blouse, managing to free her breasts without ripping the delicate cotton. Her bra fastened in the front and after a second of careful tugging, Caleb filled his palm with silky flesh. He rolled one taut peak between his finger and thumb, just the way she liked it.

Rosie arched her body and moaned into his mouth.

Pleasure point two . . .

"Oh, God, Caleb." Her voice shook; her pelvis thrust and ground against his more-than-ready erection. "Please . . ."

He didn't need any further prompting.

Crazed with need, he released her long enough to strip off his clothes, as she yanked at her jeans. Clothing flew everywhere in their frenzy to get naked, and then finally—*thank God*—they were skin on skin.

Her curves had filled out in all the right places, and he'd never wanted a woman as badly as he wanted Rosemary. Caleb slid down her body to taste one creamy breast. His tongue laved and his teeth nipped at the plump, pink tip. With a gasp she thrust her fingers into his hair, tugging him closer as he moved to her other breast and gave it the same loving attention. He trailed his mouth lower and her flesh quivered as he explored every lovely inch laid out before him. When he flicked his tongue in the hollow of her belly button, she sighed his name.

Pleasure spot three.

It might have been six years, but he still knew what Rosie liked in bed, and he was determined to give her exactly what she needed.

The silky red curls between her thighs enticed him unbearably and he slid two fingers inside her snug heat. She was so wet and ready, and he wanted to play longer, locating all those pleasure spots he'd yet to explore. But if he didn't get inside her in the next thirty seconds he wouldn't survive.

Rosemary must have had the same thought, because she gripped his neck and urged him closer. "Please, Caleb. I need you."

As desperately as he wanted to plunge deep, he fought to clear his desire-fogged brain, long enough to remember protection. Six years ago, stupidity and horniness got both of them in trouble, though Rosemary bore the consequences. He wouldn't do that to her again. *Not until it's completely right between us. Not until we're ready.*

"Condom," he panted in her ear. "Wait."

She nodded as he fumbled through the pocket of his jeans, located his wallet, and dug out a crumpled packet that thankfully had remained sealed and intact. A few seconds later he'd sheathed himself.

Caleb rose over her as she parted her legs, enticing him to settle against her slick entrance and edge inside a scant inch. Her breath caught on a gasp as he slowly pushed inside her warmth, his gaze locked on her beautiful face, tunneling his fingers through her hair as the words he rasped broke on a groan. "I've missed you, Rosie."

He paused, lifting her hips to meld their flesh completely, and felt his cock throb wildly at the soft cry she released.

"Oh, Caleb. I—I've missed you, too." Her legs curved tightly around his waist and she clung to him, her nails pressing into his back. For a second she looked dazed, as if she couldn't quite believe what they were doing together. Then she gave him a gorgeous smile and wriggled her hips. "Now move."

He dropped his face to her shoulder on a shaky chuckle. "Yes, ma'am."

Maybe she hesitated for one tiny moment. Maybe she was making a big mistake. Rosemary wasn't sure. All she knew was the rightness of Caleb, in her arms, inside her body.

Six long years of loneliness crumbled into dust as she felt him, big and hard, moving with her in a sensual dance she'd never quite forgotten. So familiar, she had to blink back the tears and press her lips together to keep from sobbing out how much she'd truly missed him.

There'd never been anyone but him. How could there be? Caleb Johnson had owned her soul from the very beginning and nobody else ever stood a flicker of a chance.

She curled her hands along his shoulder blades as his thrusts came faster, dug deeper. His fingers would probably leave bruises on her hips, but she didn't care. Each heated breath he panted into her neck, every broken endearment he huffed in her ear, pushed her need higher, made her skin tighten and prickle. There wasn't room for anything else. All her frustration over the unbalanced situation between them, any insecurity she felt for her son's sake . . . it simply evaporated into nothing when Caleb covered her mouth in a scalding kiss that rocked her senseless.

"So good—so tight—Jesus, Rosie," he groaned as their lips parted. His hair hung in damp disarray around his lean, tanned face; under her hands his muscles bunched and released as he drove her higher still.

Tension ramped her body into a fierce arch that made her grip him hard enough to choke off his air supply. In answer, Caleb caught the curve of her neck between his teeth and bit down as his hands jerked her hips tighter against his driving thrusts.

She broke, shattering in a convulsive orgasm, muffling her scream in his shoulder. Clinging frantically, she rode out her climax as Caleb pinned her to the mattress and shuddered through his own release. His chest heaved as he fought for breath; his hands had found hers and their fingers twined together as if they both needed an anchor in a storm that seemed to go on and on.

So much like what they'd had between them years earlier. And she couldn't have stemmed the overflowing tears that dampened the hair at her temples. She didn't even try; she let them fall while her heart finally calmed and her muscles relaxed, her body going limp beneath his.

Seconds later, she felt Caleb slump in her arms, sated; another memory she'd missed like crazy. How he'd simply melt over her when the last tiny shivers worked through his large frame, and their damp skin fused together amongst tangled sheets. The best feeling in the world, and here they were again. She loved it.

She loved him.

As Caleb turned his lips to the curve of her shoulder and kissed the place he'd bitten, she realized it was pointless to fight the inevitable. He was her son's daddy. The connection between them hadn't lessened at all over the years, and it didn't seem to matter what he might have done while on the rodeo circuit or how many women he'd probably slept with.

What mattered was now, this minute, and what they built together as a result. Even as she admitted it to herself, Rosemary had a feeling the toughest, at least for her, would be reestablishing trust. But she was willing to try. She slipped her hands from his loosened grip and twined her arms around his neck, holding him close, and let herself drift.

Emitting a soft protest as he moved away slightly, she quieted when he murmured, "Be right back." A soft rustle of the sheets reminded her Caleb needed to dispose of the protection he'd used.

He returned quickly, gathering her into his arms. With a sigh, Rosemary fell into a light doze.

Later—it might have been minutes or hours—Caleb roused her by scattering heated kisses over her breasts. Then he murmured, "I want to stay the night," against one puckered nipple.

Rosemary turned her head on the pillow as he moved his mouth to hers and nipped briefly, before facing her with sleepy eyes and cheeks already shadowed with dark blond stubble.

So sexy; so very male. Caleb Johnson, in a nutshell. *And he's all mine.* At least for the moment. Still, she tried it out in a whisper, her lips touching his. "Mine."

"Yeah, I am." He deepened the kiss, his tongue stroking hers. The moment spun out in the warm, quiet room, the give and take of their mouths echoing in the resurgence of passion that had him hardening against her belly.

She arched, mindless with desire. "Caleb. Yes."

"Yes, I can stay?"

His attempt at lighthearted banter didn't fool her one bit, because she could all but taste the need pouring from him as he slipped a hand beneath her and held her tightly.

In the midst of overwhelming emotion, it seemed cold and mechanical to ask the obvious question, but she regained enough of her common sense to whisper, "Do you have more . . ." She couldn't finish, burying her heated face in his neck.

His shoulders shook beneath her cheek. He was laughing at her! She wanted to slug him, but his body felt so good, she couldn't bring herself to pull away.

"Baby, I've got plenty of, um, opportunities to rock your world," Caleb assured her solemnly, then slid against her suggestively.

She shivered, moaned, shivered again, before reaching for his cock and palming it firmly. "Then I guess you'd better get that endless supply, cowboy . . . and stay." Her breath snagged on a moan as his flesh seemed to leap and pulse in her hand. "God, Caleb." She coiled herself around him. "Don't go, never go . . ."

"I'm not going anywhere." He covered her lips with a hard, wild kiss.

"Mommy. Daddy. I'm hungry." The childish voice piped up close to his ear, accompanied by a cough and a sneeze. Caleb stirred reluctantly, disoriented for a few moments.

Daylight flooded the room. *Rosemary's bedroom.* In a flash it all came back to him; the loving they'd shared, interspersed with an hour here and there of exhausted sleep. Only to awaken in each other's arms and do it all over again.

Then he remembered how he'd ended up here in the first place. Carson was doing much better but still not completely out of the woods from the pneumonia he'd suffered.

Caleb eased his arm from under Rosemary's sleeping form. She muttered softly and curled herself around her pillow as he sat up in bed and beckoned to his son. "Morning, buddy. Hungry, huh? I can fix that." Belatedly he glanced down to assure the sheet covered his naked ass. *Whew, safe.*

"How?" Carson crawled onto the bed and settled into Caleb's arms. His soft red hair was tangled, wayward ends sticking up all over. With his cheeks rosy from sleep, bright eyed and eager for the day to begin, he looked like an adorable, slightly mischievous cherub.

Caleb snatched him close and mock-growled into his sweet-smelling neck, eliciting a torrent of giggles as Carson squirmed away from the beard stubble Caleb tickled him with. "I happen to be the world-famous blueberry pancake king."

"Nuh-uh! Guys don't make pancakes. Girls do!" Carson curled his little fingers into claws and went right for Caleb's armpits in retaliation.

"Uh-huh. Guys make the best pancakes, just wait and see." Though he'd never been ticklish in his life, Caleb emitted loud, chortling sounds as his son dug in with gusto. "If I promise to cook up some amazing pancakes, will you stop tickling me and help me make your mommy breakfast in bed?"

"You bet!" Carson jumped to the floor and grabbed for Caleb's hand. "Hurry! Before Mommy wakes up."

"I have to get dressed first, champ. Okay? And do some stuff in the bathroom. Meet me in the kitchen." Caleb bent close to his son's ear and whispered, "We'll start on 'Operation Pancake,' post-haste." He cracked a grin as Carson whooped and ran for the door. His bare feet slapped along the hallway and stomped down the stairs. The sound brought a lump of emotion to Caleb's throat that he fought to swallow down.

I want to wake up like this for the rest of my life.

Rubbing at suddenly stinging eyes, he smoothed the sheet away, then jerked in surprise as a warm, slender hand stroked over his arm. Turning, Caleb brought Rosemary close as she wriggled to his side of the bed and climbed into his lap, the same as Carson had done.

"So, surprise pancakes? Really?" She nuzzled his cheek, before closing her mouth over his in a delicious kiss.

They shared nibbles and soft, morning caresses, as more sunlight poured into the room and the sound of little-boy feet clomping down the hall reminded them they weren't alone upstairs. Everything felt right in the world, and he couldn't remember when he'd been so happy.

Caleb eased away first, with a lingering kiss to one sweetly puckered breast. "My pancakes will make your tummy weep."

"For joy? Or with heartburn?" she retorted cheekily.

He gave her bare bottom a cuff. "Let me up, smartass, and you'll see."

The kitchen rang with laughter as Caleb and Carson made a shambles of mixing and cooking pancakes. Rosemary had run out of blueberries a week ago, so her son decided nothing but apples would do as a substitute. Worried her boy might actually try talking Caleb into letting him have a paring knife, Rosemary positioned herself on a kitchen chair and kept an eye on both her men. They balked at her interference but were mollified when she vowed not to lift a finger.

Keeping her promise wasn't easy especially after Carson dropped his third egg on the floor, and the flour canister exploded when Caleb knocked it over. She slapped a hand over her mouth to keep in her protest as well as her chuckles, resigned to spending a good hour cleaning up their mess.

Twenty sloppy minutes later, they sat down to surprisingly delicious, fluffy pancakes packed with apples and cinnamon. Carson crammed them in as fast as his fork could cut them, and Rosemary sighed at the taste.

"Yummy. I'm impressed, Caleb. Where'd you learn to make pancakes like this?"

"It's the beer," he replied casually, swallowing a huge bite.

She almost dropped her juice glass. "You put beer in them? You can't feed beer pancakes to a five-year-old! What were you thinking?"

"I'm thinking you're pretty easy to rile up, Carmichael." He offered a smug snort. "Not only do you not have beer in your fridge, but you sat there and watched us make them. Did you see a beer bottle anywhere?"

"Um—" Rosemary felt her cheeks heat and she rubbed at them. As Carson giggled wildly, she mumbled, "Now who's a smartass?"

After threatening to tie her to the chair if she tried to help clean up, Caleb settled Carson with a sink full of soapy water and what unbreakable utensils they'd used. As Carson stood on his little stepstool and played at washing the dishes, Caleb scooted a chair close to her and nibbled at her mouth. "Let's take him to Hawthorn, let him work off some of that energy. We can stop at Sonic and get some corn dogs and onion rings."

"You just ate. How can you think of food?" But Rosemary tilted her head to give him better access to her neck, loving the feel of his calloused fingers trailing along her arms.

"I also just had sex. Well, last night," he teased softly so Carson wouldn't hear. "How can I think of getting you naked and under me? I just can, baby."

"Shh, jeez!" She slapped a hand over his mouth. "You think he's not listening but I promise you, little boys hear everything."

Caleb kissed her palm. "Let's spend the day in Hawthorn."

The persuasive tone in his sexy voice left Rosemary unable to form a single objection. She didn't even try. Instead, she slid her hand from his mouth to the back of his neck and pulled him in for a fast, moist bite to his full bottom lip.

"Okay."

Chapter Nine

It'd been ten years or more since Caleb had hung out at Hawthorn. The park sat about three miles outside of Dustin, a sprawling conglomerate of public swimming pools, several carnival rides including a restored carousel, and a children's museum that was a kid's dream.

He could remember taking Rosemary here once, during the few daylight hours when they had actually climbed out of bed for something other than sex. Even then, he'd found ways to ambush her with caresses and kisses. Behind the main cabana at the adult pool. Under the bleachers on the softball field while the Dustin Lil' Wranglers played their hearts out. Up against one of the mammoth cottonwoods scattered through the park, his lips devouring that sweet spot between her neck and her shoulder, bared by the cute little sundress she'd worn. He'd had her hands pinned to the rough bark over her head, one of her long, shapely legs wound around his waist, when a park official strolled by and busted them.

"You okay, Daddy? You kinda made a noise." Carson's sweet chirp dragged Caleb out of the sexual fog of memories and the groan he'd released under his breath.

He looked over at Rosemary's *cut-that-out* expression and then into his son's concerned face. "Just hungry, buddy. It's been so long since our pancakes, right?"

"It's been two whole hours," Rosemary inserted dryly.

"Yeah, but you know pancakes. Two hours later and you're starving."

She snickered. "That's Chinese food, not pancakes."

"Same difference." Sweeping up his giggling son in one arm, Caleb tugged Rosemary forward with his free hand. "Come on, let's hit the merry-go-round before we eat so we won't get pukey."

"I want the camel! I want the camel!" Carson bounced madly, his fingers twisted into Caleb's shirt collar. "Daddy, the camel, okay?"

"You got it, son. As long as nobody else is riding on it."

A light breeze ruffled the edges of Rosemary's long, loose curls as she walked beside him. She wore faded Levi's that clung to every luscious curve and a thin cotton blouse with no sleeves, the unbuttoned ends tied beneath her perfect breasts. Each time he eyed that expanse of creamy pale midriff she'd left bare, Caleb broke out in a sweat. A pair of dusty, beat-up red leather Dingos with squared off toes peeked from the frayed hem of her jeans. He vaguely remembered them from years ago and couldn't believe she'd kept them all this time. Without a speck of lipstick or anything else on her face, she looked no more than sixteen.

Then she glanced sideways and gave him a smile, lips parted slightly and showing a flash of straight, white teeth.

Unable to look away from her beauty, every muscle in his body tightened and clenched with need. *This woman.* Only Rosemary. There'd never be anyone else for him.

When Carson wriggled to get down, then tugged on his hand, Caleb blinked and shook his head. His cheeks heated like a teenager, and from just a single smoldering glance from the fiery redhead standing so close to him.

He broke the contact between them, squatting next to his son whose excitement had him bouncing in his scuffed hi-top sneakers. "You got a bee up your butt, partner?" he teased gently.

Carson waved his arms in a childish frenzy. "Daddy, the camel!" He squirmed impatiently.

The music from a piping calliope floated on the air, and Caleb turned toward the familiar tune. There sat the carousel, an antique marvel of what modern restoration could accomplish. When Caleb was a kid, the carousel worked but its colors had been faded, with the tips of equine ears broken off and paint missing from saddles and muzzles. Somebody had spent a shitload of money to bring the ride to its former glory. It now sparkled in the sun, packed with joyous children riding their favorite animals with happy abandon, while their parents waved and snapped pictures.

"Can we go? Please?" Carson tugged at both their hands.

Rosemary's laughter floated across the air as she allowed Carson to drag her forward, while Caleb pretended to protest and lag behind. More determined than ever, their son pulled harder until they all stood at the chainlink fence circling the carousel. He would have bolted through the gate if Rosemary hadn't grabbed the back of his shirt.

"Carson, calm down. We have to buy tickets, then wait our turn." She knelt and traced a gentle finger along his pouting lower lip. "That camel isn't going anywhere, honey. You and Daddy get the tickets, and I'll hold your place in line." She lifted his chin. "Okay?"

"Okay," he mumbled, then gave her a hopeful look. "Can I ride as much as I want?"

Caleb couldn't contain his snort of laughter. "What an operator." He ruffled his son's soft curls. "Come on, let's go buy some tickets. Maybe a roll of them." His promised got Carson squealing ecstatically and jumping up and down.

As Caleb grinned at his son's antics, Rosemary leaned over and gave him a lingering kiss, a fast, hot flick of her tongue, and a parting shot.

"Sucker."

Waiting in line at the carousel, Rosemary pressed a hand to her fluttering stomach. The kiss she'd given Caleb had been meant as a silly tease, but even a touch of that mouth on hers made her center clutch. She sucked in a steadying breath just as a hand tapped her shoulder.

"Hey, Rosie! How've you been?" Miranda Benson, nicknamed 'Mimi' since childhood, stood behind her in line, three giggling boys holding onto the conch belt cinching her narrow cowgirl hips.

Mimi had made the women's rodeo circuit in Dustin and Cheyenne during her teen years, whittling the baby fat from her body like only an extreme workout of riding and roping could do. Younger by two years, Mimi's sister Dwana had followed in her footsteps, taking it even further and becoming a professional roper on the circuit. Mimi had dropped out to marry, and her husband Frank moved the family to Cheyenne last year.

Rosemary had lost touch with both Mimi and Dwana, catching up only here and there when Mimi and the boys came to town.

She gave Mimi a quick hug. "Hi, Mimi. I've been good. You?"

"Been good. Busy." She blew honey blonde curls off her forehead.

"Where's Frank?" Rosemary hadn't seen him walk up.

"Trucking as usual." Mimi rolled her eyes. "Big load to Montana. He'll be back tomorrow." Her smile held the weariness as well as the fortitude of a long-haul trucker's wife.

Rosemary stood back and grinned at the trio of chubby-cheeked faces peering at her. "I can't believe how big your boys have grown." She opened her arms to collect the adorable herd, identical triplets with their mother's sky-blue eyes and their dad's black hair. As the boys huddled close in a wriggling snuggle, she glanced up at Mimi. "Are you here for the day?"

"Yep. There's nothing like this in Cheyenne, damn it all. And we promised the boys." Mimi tousled two heads and snickered at their indignant groans. "Little buggers are starved as usual. But they begged to ride first, then we're going to Sonic." She looked around curiously. "Where's that cutie of yours? Are you here all day, too?"

"Well, I—" Rosemary didn't get any farther, because Mimi's jaw unhinged in a gape. Tensing, Rosemary looked over her shoulder as Caleb and Carson strolled along the carousel boundary, hand in hand.

"Is that—oh, my—um . . ." Mimi turned a shocked face to her. "Caleb Johnson." She flicked him another glance. "When did he blow in? Are you two together?"

Rosemary sighed as she released the boys so they could run to the fence and watch the carousel spin. "He got in about ten days ago. It's kind of a long story, Mimi. I guess you could say we're trying it out to see if it fits." She scraped her hair back from her face with fingers that held a tremble. "Carson adores him."

"Does he know who Caleb is?"

"Oh, yes." She gestured helplessly. "What else can I do? I have to give this a chance."

"Yeah." Mimi nodded in empathy. "I get it, believe me. You remember what Frank and I went through. I knew damned well the man didn't want to get married even with three babies on the way. My daddy threatened him with a shotgun." She winked. "It wasn't loaded, thank God. Of course Frank loved me back then but he was an immature ass. He's grown up a lot." She squeezed Rosemary's arm reassuringly. "I always liked Caleb even if he was a wild one. He has steady eyes."

Before Rosemary could respond, Carson spotted them and screeched, "Mimi Moo!" He broke from Caleb's grip and tore up to Mimi, flinging his arms wide. With a laugh, she dropped to her knees and cuddled him tightly.

"Mimi Moo?" Caleb murmured as he stepped to Rosemary's side and slipped an arm around her.

She had to chuckle a bit. "You remember Miranda, right? Carson called her that silly nickname because of the calf she and the triplets raised for 4-H last year. It kind of stuck."

Mimi got to her feet, and assessed Caleb appraisingly. "As I live and breathe, he's back." She gave his cowboy hat a tug and it fell over his forehead. "Good to see you, Caleb. Whatcha think of this short stack?" She tickled Carson under his ear, making him squeal.

Caleb thumbed his hat back into place. His lips twitched. "He's okay in a pinch."

When Carson launched himself against his legs, Caleb swung him over his shoulder like a sack of feed. "Kind of scrawny but we'll take care of that." He swatted his son's backside and Carson shrieked with laughter, hanging upside down. He dug ten mischievous fingers in the vicinity of his daddy's ribs and the two of them tussled while Rosemary grinned like a star-struck fangirl. She couldn't help herself.

Caleb pulled Carson right side up and hefted him in one arm. He turned to study Mimi's boys, who were shoving each other noisily as they ran up to their mother. "There's a rowdy bunch. Yours?"

She nodded and reined them in with practiced hands.

"How old are you cowpokes?" he asked the boys.

"Four!" they hollered in unison. Mimi winced, but her expression held plenty of pride.

"Miranda, I'm impressed. Good on ya." Caleb tipped his hat to her and she loosed a deep chortle.

"Same goes, Johnson. You've got yourself a terrific kid. I'm glad to see you back." She leaned in and added in a not-so-subtle murmur, "Hang smart, y'hear?"

Rosemary groaned, "Mimi, for cripe's sake."

Winking, Mimi touched her arm. "I've got an idea. Why don't you let us take the little stinker for a while? He can jump on some rides with the boys and have lunch with us. Probably Sonic." She nodded toward Caleb and they both watched him balance Carson on the tops of his boots. He shuffled his feet, bouncing Carson up and sideways, eliciting a fit of giggles.

Rosemary parted her lips to demur as Mimi raised her voice to catch Carson's attention. "Hey, squirt, wanna hang out with the boys and chow down on some corn dogs over at Sonic?"

"Yeah! Onion rings, too?" Carson jumped off Caleb's feet and ran up to Rosemary. "Can I, Mommy?"

"Oh, I don't know, honey—" As she vacillated, unsure, Carson turned to his father with a child's innate knowledge of how to pit one parent against the other.

"Daddy, can I, please?" The soft plea in their son's voice was lethal, and Caleb wouldn't withstand its appeal any more than she could. Behind her, Mimi coughed rudely.

"Ask Mommy, and what she says, goes. Okay?" Caleb hunkered down to their son's level. "And you can have all the tickets we bought as long as you share with the boys. But you have to be really good and do everything Mimi says. You understand?" At Carson's frantic nod, Caleb squinted up at Rosemary from beneath his hat. "What d'ya think, warden? Should we spring the kid?"

She could no more resist those bedroom eyes of his, any more than the puppy-dog looks Carson bombarded her with. "Oh, all right. But if I hear of one single problem, you're in for it." She braced herself for Carson's whoop of joy and the impact of his sturdy little body against hers.

A few minutes later the Bensons were off, with Carson holding two of the triplets' hands and Mimi clutching the third boy. Probably Kenny, who she recalled was the most rambunctious of the three. Kevin and Keith would willingly stick by Carson.

As Rosemary waved at Mimi, she felt a strong arm slip around her waist. Caleb pulled her into his chest and she shivered at the feel of those hard muscles at her back.

His free hand nudged her hair out of the way, then trailed along her neck. His lips followed, brushing over her skin, the tenor of his breathing accelerating when she relaxed against his body in surrender. Loving the way he nibbled and licked, Rosemary refused to think of who might be around, watching or judging her. It didn't really concern anyone but them.

"Let's take a walk," he whispered unsteadily in her ear.

She could feel the mad thump of her heart. Everywhere their bodies touched, heat was generating, blistering what remained of her common sense.

I don't give a damn at all. She turned in his arms and met his seeking lips. Against them she moaned, "Hell, yeah."

Chapter Ten

His hand warm on the back of her neck, Caleb guided Rosemary along the nature path connecting one side of the park to the other. His thumb stroked gently under her hair, over her ultra-sensitive nape. She could have easily melted in her boots.

When she swayed slightly, Caleb's knowing chuckle stiffened her spine and she flashed him a glance, wavering between irritation and affection. *Overconfident smartass.*

Though she loved being alone with him, a mother's natural worry kicked in and she found she couldn't completely relax. It wasn't so much a safety concern. Miranda would care for Carson as one of her own and Rosemary fully trusted her. It was more than that. Despite their reconnection the night before and a new understanding growing between them, she still couldn't completely trust Caleb to stick around for Carson. That made every hour with him as part of a family unit precious. Lord knew, she wanted to trust him. She wasn't quite there yet.

Then she told herself to stop being an idiot and just enjoy what she could.

They passed the adult pool area with its heated Jacuzzi, the water a comfortable temperature year-round. "We should have brought our swimsuits," she commented idly.

Caleb snagged one of her hands and swung it between them, like he used to do years ago. "We can always come back another day, Rosie." He tugged her closer and brushed a teasing kiss across her nose. "Or sneak in after dark and go skinny-dipping."

"Oh, yes. Great idea especially since last year they upped the security system with about a hundred extra cameras." She gave his shoulder a playful shove. "It'd be all over Youtube."

"Hey, I'd download it. Late at night when I'm lonely." Caleb yanked her up hard against his chest. "Lucky for me, I've got the real thing right here." In the shade of a cottonwood he sucked gently at her throat, and everything went right out of her head, wiped clean by those warm, full lips and tongue stroking fire on her skin.

With a breathy sigh Rosemary tunneled her fingers through his hair, fisting the heavy strands, encouraging him to take anything he wanted. On a public path like this, half of Dustin could mosey on by at any time and gawk at them. She couldn't bring herself to care.

She pulled until he raised his head enough that she could kiss him. Then she swallowed his mouth, his tongue, and the thick groan he uttered as his hands dug under her backside and hoisted her high, easing her against the cottonwood trunk.

"Wrap your legs around me," he demanded hoarsely, and she made her rubbery limbs obey.

Tree bark poked her back, but she barely acknowledged its scrape. Her head, her heart and soul so full of Caleb, what he did to her . . . nothing else mattered. And those small remnants of mistrust—that he'd up and leave when it suited him—shattered under the pure strength of his body against hers, hot and vital. But she felt the tremor in his fingers where they gripped her, the shiver that moved up his spine when she slid her tongue over the firm flesh along his jaw. And she knew what exploded between them affected him as much as it did her.

"Ah, Rosie . . . I'd give anything to have you naked right now." The words burst from his throat, low and rough. His hips had begun a not-so-subtle thrust against her center, the hard ridge beneath his button-fly hitting her just right.

Rosemary could almost feel her eyes roll back in her head. When Caleb propped her on one brawny arm and snaked his free hand inside her gapping shirt collar, she gnawed her bottom lip, hard. It was either that, or scream loudly enough to flush birds right out of the cottonwood branches above.

He flicked open a few buttons, his fingers shaky, then hissed out a curse when he found bare skin. "God almighty, baby. How could I not know you've been braless all day?" He bent his head and covered her nipple with hungry lips.

Her lids fluttered shut, then snapped wide open as she looked around furtively for others on the walking path. Though she didn't see anyone, the sane and yet-unscrambled portion of her brain told her it was just a matter of time before someone caught them doing illicit, probably illegal acts in public. Still, she couldn't help but cup his neck and keep him close as the feel of his mouth and tongue sent her into boneless submission. And she needed to watch him do it. She had to see.

She shuddered when Caleb met her gaze with hooded passion, his lips rosy and eager against her pale flesh.

A beam of sunlight filtered through the cottonwood leaves and set a fiery glow over Rosemary's tangled hair. Caleb had lost track of how many kisses he'd scattered over her bared skin. The urge to strip her naked and take her against the damned tree grew with each sigh she uttered in the quiet surrounding this section of the park. And her hands, Christ . . . what the woman could do to him with those soft, pretty hands should be outlawed. He leaned in for another kiss, shifting her body even closer, choking out a growl when her breasts pushed against his tee shirt and her legs clamped his hips.

"Grandma, cotton candy!" The childish screech echoed along the path. Breaking their kiss, Caleb looked up and spotted an elderly couple about seventy-five yards away, meandering slowly, swinging a little girl between them. Right now they were too far out to see much of anything. But the park only got more crowded in the afternoon and early evening when various free concerts started up and a few food booths opened for business.

He sidled along the tree and held Rosemary steady as she eased her feet back to the ground. The little wriggling movements she made along the way just about killed him. Caleb groaned softly and pressed his forehead to her shoulder. He could feel her shake as she formed a chuckle.

"It's not funny." He discreetly adjusted himself.

Rosemary shook her head as if to clear it. "You recall the last time we got rousted from this very park for necking in public?" She swiftly buttoned up as he shielded her from Grandpa and Grandma's steady advance down the path. By the time the old geezers reached the heavier copse of cottonwoods, she was tucked and smoothed out, leaning against the trunk, the picture of innocence. Caleb nodded a greeting as the towheaded little girl—about Carson's age—dragged her grandparents toward the shack selling cotton candy.

"She'll wear them out in no time." He snared her wrist and pulled her in for a fast, voracious kiss.

Rosemary came willingly enough but a touch of hesitancy in her response told him, better than words, their bubble of intimacy had probably popped for the day. Even so, he had to ask. "You all right, Rosie?" He brought her hand to his face and held it there, inexplicably relieved when she stroked him gently.

"I'm good. But I think we should head back to the carousel and find Carson. It's getting late and I still have to figure out dinner and scrub about ten pounds of park crud off our son." Rising on tiptoe, she brushed her lips over his cheek.

Caleb cradled her tenderly, thinking that of all the wonderful events of today, all the laughter and kisses, the sweetest had to be the words, 'our son' coming from those gorgeous lips now pressed to his cheek. He wondered if she knew how deeply she'd touched his heart.

He wondered if she knew he'd never let her go.

They collected a very excited boy on the short path between the carousel and the picnic area. Carson's hair stuck up in wild tufts, his plaid shirt half in, half out of his cargo shorts, clutching a stuffed alligator almost bigger than him. Mimi and the triplets trailed behind him, all grinning widely. The boys' faces were smeared with what looked like cotton candy and mustard.

"Look, Daddy!" Carson shoved the silly looking purple gator at Caleb. "Mimi Moo and me won Fred!"

Caleb held the gator up for inspection. It wore a bright yellow cowboy hat and hot pink hi-top sneakers on each foot. "This is quite the stylish lizard, huh?" Then he blinked down at his son. "'Fred?'"

"Don't ask," Mimi snorted. She opened her arms to Carson. "C'mere, short stack, and give me some sugar."

Giggling, Carson took a running leap and hung on Mimi like a little monkey, his arms and legs wound tight. He gave her a smacking kiss. "Thanks, Aunt Mimi. For helping me win Fred."

"And?" Rosemary prodded gently.

"And for feeding me, and letting me ride the camel for like a hundred times." He laid his head on her shoulder trustingly. "Can I come see you sometime? And play with the guys?"

She swung him around a few times and got him squealing. "You betcha, cowboy. Anytime. But make sure it's okay with your folks. Don't just jump a club car and ride those rails to Cheyenne, y'hear?"

As Carson's eyes got big at the mention of stowing away on a train, Rosemary groaned. "Oh, jeez. Don't give him any ideas." She knelt and scooped Mimi's herd into a communal snuggle, laughing as they peppered her cheeks with sticky kisses.

Carson wriggled from Mimi's arms and ran to Caleb. "Can we ride the rails, Daddy? Like a hobo?"

Caleb coughed out a chuckle. "What do you know about hobos?" He grabbed for his adorable boy, deftly flipping him upside down, then shared a knowing look with Rosemary. "You buy the tickets, we'll ride in style all the way to Cheyenne, deal?"

"Okay!" Carson flapped his arms like a bird. "Can you carry me this way?" His voice sounded garbled from the rush of blood to his face.

Caleb swung him right side up and planted him firmly on the ground. "No can do, tough guy. Not upside down. But you can piggy." He knelt and thumbed toward his back. "Hop on."

Carson didn't need to be invited twice. He clambered up and clung. Caleb handed Fred to Rosemary, then slipped his hands under Carson's legs to stabilize him, while Rosemary used Fred's sneaker-covered paw to wave goodbye at Mimi and the boys.

Heading for the parking lot, Caleb bounced Carson with every other stride as Rosemary waltzed in circles with Fred in her arms. Their son giggled all the way to the car, the best sound in the world.

"I'm in the mood to cook," Rosemary announced, as Caleb pulled up to one of a handful of traffic lights in Dustin. "Maybe fried chicken and cheesy mashed potatoes. What do you think? You guys hungry for real food?"

In the back seat, Carson immediately started jumping up and down. "Yeah, yeah! Chicken and po!"

"Sit still, buddy," Caleb warned. "And put your seat belt back on, okay? Don't want you flying out the window."

"Aww, gee." But he did as he was told, sitting quietly. Caleb gave him a commiserating grin toward the rearview mirror, understanding how hard it was for a kid to sit still.

When Rosemary hooked her hand over his thigh, he turned the grin into a comical leer and murmured, "I could go for chicken. Maybe a breast."

"Shh, jeez." She pinched him in a tender spot, then rubbed it in apology. "We'll have to stop by Safeway. My supplies are pathetically low. You remember where it is? On Sprig, near the bakery."

"Yep. Hasn't been a whole lot of changes in Dustin, you know." Caleb made the turn onto Sprig Street, then dropped a hand from the steering wheel to cover her fingers and hike them higher on his thigh. "Only the important stuff changed and for the better," he stressed.

"Whatever do you mean, Mr. Johnson?" She wore a demure expression but her cheeks had flushed.

He slowed down to enter the Safeway parking lot and whipped into a slot next to a cart return. Killing the engine, Caleb leaned in and pressed a kiss to her mouth, warm and soft under his lips. Before Carson could start squirming impatiently, he murmured, "All you've given me, that's the most important change of all." He cupped her chin tenderly. "Carson. A chance to prove myself to you." His voice dropped to a rasp. "Your love."

She swallowed convulsively. "Caleb—"

"Mommy, let's go!" Carson hollered from the rear.

Caleb shuddered out a sigh as he pulled away. "You heard the peanut gallery back there. Let's go chase down a chicken."

Inside, Rosemary consulted the shopping list she'd slapped together before they left Hawthorn. Caleb tossed Carson in a cart and wheeled him up and down the aisles, making silly engine noises to the delight of their son. Each item on the list was passed off to Carson who carefully laid them in the cart, then did his best to keep his feet from squashing anything. In between grocery placement, Carson kept up a chattering commentary ranging from multiple corn dogs at Sonic to how many times he rode the carousel without throwing up.

Caleb made appropriate noises of approval while Rosemary muttered, "If he doesn't puke in the middle of the night we'll all be lucky."

"Well, if he does, I'll clean it up." Caleb ran caressing fingers under her hair and enjoyed the shiver that swept over her from his touch.

Her eyes met his, soft amber, tinged with a promise. "Let's get the rest and go home. I'm hungry."

"So am I, baby." But he wasn't talking about food.

At the checkout counter, Carson stood in the cart and craned his neck like a bird dog. "Where's Daddy?"

"Sit down before you fall down," Rosemary scolded gently, then handed him a can of baking powder to keep him occupied. "Here, help me unload. And your daddy got a phone call."

Actually, that call worried her a bit, not to mention the look on Caleb's face when he checked the display. But he'd flashed her a quick smile before swiping the screen, then put it to his ear and stepped away to take the call. She and Carson had continued shopping.

Now she dug bills from her wallet, relieved she carried enough money. Usually she only used a credit card if she absolutely had to. As she tucked her change into her purse she heard Carson screech, "Uncle Mason!"

Oh, just great. Rosemary loved her brother a lot, but lately he'd been pissing her off with his poor attitude toward Caleb and refusal to believe his once-best friend could change for the better. She didn't have time to deal with Mason's crap, especially in public. And by his determined expression as he strode in her direction, she just knew the idiot would say something to make her mad.

"Hey there, Lil' Tuff." Mason yanked on a lock of her son's hair. "Where've you been all day?" He directed the question at Carson but his focus remained on her as she loaded the bags in the cart.

She bit back on her impatience and pinned a smile in place as Carson chirped, "We went to the park! I ate five corn dogs at Sonic, and saw Mimi Moo, and we won Fred, and Daddy let me ride the camel a hundred times—"

Mason interrupted abruptly with the only thing he'd heard in that whole mess of chatter. "Daddy?" He turned to Rosemary with a thundering frown. "You've been with *him* all day?" His voice lowered to a snarl. "What the hell, Rosie!"

She hastened forward, edging him away from Carson's curiosity as he knelt in the cart and stared at them. "Mason, you can just shut up right now." She stabbed his chest with two fingers, unwilling to back down. "None of this is your business. What I do or where I go with Caleb isn't anything to you."

Turning to Carson, she said brightly, "Hang on to the cart, sweetheart. Let's get this stuff out to the car and wait for Daddy." Without another word, Rosemary shoved the cart through the exit doors toward the parking lot.

She hoped her brother would stay in the store, but Mason predictably followed her outside, blocking her path as she moved to unload the bags. "I got news for you, Rosie. This *is* my business. Who took you to your doctor appointments and loaned you money when you had to quit working? Who listened to you cry at night and lent you a shoulder? Huh?"

Rosemary dashed impatiently at wet cheeks, angry her blasted brother could get her riled enough to tear up. Thank God Carson was already in the car and didn't see. "Don't you dare throw that up to me. I paid you back the money. I thanked you over and over for everything you did for me, Mason. I'm a grown woman now. I make my own choices and right now I choose to see how Caleb does as a father. I choose to give my son the chance to know his daddy."

"He'll stomp on your heart, Rosemary. After he gets what he wants, he'll leave as soon as his leg's steady enough to jump on the next rodeo stupid enough to take the entry money." Mason scraped one hand down his face, then waved it toward the car where Carson sat. "What about him? How hurt do you think that boy'll feel when Mr. Rodeo King takes off? Because he will. It's what he does."

"I don't want to hear any more." She pushed by her brother, dragging the cart to the nearest return slot and slamming it in. For a few seconds she stood with her back to the car, striving to regain some sort of composure. If she didn't, she'd likely kill him. At the very least she'd say things she'd someday regret.

With a deep breath she turned and stared at Mason. His face was still flushed with anger, yet she could read concern, the kind you'd expect from a big, overprotective brother. He couldn't help it, any more than she could help resenting his attitude.

She probably owed him some kind of apology. "Mason, look—"

Caleb's sudden appearance interrupted her. "What's going on?" He stepped to her side, cell phone in hand, looking from her to Mason, who was visibly bristling. "Everything okay?"

Mason surged forward with a growl. "Johnson, you son of—"

"*Mason!* Enough." She felt like ripping her hair out by the roots and grinding it under her boot heel. Trying even harder for patience, Rosemary turned to Caleb. "My brother is being a jackass. He thinks you're going to break Carson's heart and leave." She cast a fulminating glare toward Mason. "I told him that would never happen."

"Oh." Caleb slowly pocketed his cell, removed his hat, and slapped it against his thigh before dropping it back on his head.

"So, who was the call from? Sounded important." Rosemary hated the tiny smidge of insecurity that had her questioning the man she knew she'd never stopped loving.

"Yeah, old *buddy*." Mason's lip curled in a faint sneer. "Who was on the phone?"

Caleb edged Rosemary away from her brother with a hand to her arm. "We should really get Carson home."

She didn't like what she saw in his eyes. "Caleb . . ." She grasped his fingers and held tightly. "Who was the call from?"

He released a short sigh and shuffled his feet, before raising worried eyes to hers. "The State Rodeo Commission."

Chapter Eleven

Caleb swallowed hard when Rosemary's eyes narrowed, her expression looking a helluva lot like her brother's. *Not good.* He needed to handle his next words very carefully if he wanted to salvage his relationship with her and Carson.

"O-okay," she said slowly, the hard look in her eyes reminding him of an ornery bull right before he climbed on for their eight-second dance. "The Rodeo Commission. And they wanted . . . what, exactly?"

Mason snorted, but otherwise remained silent. The fury in his expression said it all.

"Let's get home first, Rosie, then we can discuss the phone call." Caleb took a step forward as she pulled from his grasp.

Her hands flew up in a defensive gesture, warding him off. "No," she retorted. "Tell me now."

Caleb knew her well enough to figure she wouldn't get into the car until he'd answered her question. She was stubborn. Just one of the many things he loved about her. And yeah, damn it, he *did* love her. Had loved her from their very first kiss six years earlier, but he'd been too big of a jackass to admit it. Instead, he'd skipped town and did everything he could to put her out of his mind. *Hell.* If she left him now, it'd be his own damn fault.

Tension filled his body. He chanced losing her forever if he lied to her. It was a small miracle she'd allowed him back into her life—into her bed—as it was. He licked his suddenly dry lips. "They offered me a job as Rodeo Announcer."

Rosemary inhaled sharply. "In Cheyenne? Or on the statewide circuit?"

"Rosie—"

"Which, Caleb? Local or circuit?"

Caleb's heart beat frantically against his chest, warning him things were about to go south if he didn't do something fast. Trouble was, the offer he'd been presented had been a bit vague. He started to speak, hesitated, caught the fierce frown on Mason's face, and finally replied, "Circuit."

"And what did you tell them?" Her voice shook. She leaned against the side of the car, as if her legs weren't steady enough to hold her.

Caleb glanced past her to see Carson strapped into the back seat, playing games on Rosemary's cell phone, oblivious to the tension outside the car. Thank God, because he didn't want his son to think for one instant that he didn't rank as number one in his daddy's priorities.

The phone call had come out of left field and thrown him for a loop. His mind was still struggling with how he could have both his family *and* his career. No way was he leaving Rosie or Carson behind. But he couldn't pull his son out of school to drag him around the circuit.

Damn it! I need time to think. Time to negotiate.

Only when Rosemary made a strangling sound and spun to open the car door did he realize he'd been standing there saying nothing as he'd contemplated his options. Which completely gave her the wrong impression, like he'd really desert her again. *Hell, no.* He moved forward, intent on begging her to listen.

Mason stepped in the way, and they bumped chests. His old buddy had murder in his eyes. "Let her go, Johnson."

"Out of my way, Mason." His hands curled into fists at his sides, a rush of adrenaline coursing through him, ramping up a feeling of desperation as Rosemary slid behind the wheel of the car.

"Rosie, come on. We need to talk about this." He made a move to dart around her brother, but Mason shoved him hard in the chest with one hand, sending him back on his heels. His bad leg twinged hard, but Caleb determinately ignored it. "Rosie," he pleaded as he righted his footing, their gazes meeting for a split second.

The pain he saw reflected on her face gutted him. Pain he'd once again caused her. She slammed the door shut, starting the car.

"Wait, damn it. Rosie!"

Panic stabbed him straight through the heart as the car drove away with everything that mattered to him inside. He'd really screwed up this time.

"Just go, Johnson," Mason snapped. "Take the damn job and get the hell out of town. That's what you do best, remember? Leave."

Caleb tensed as a surge of fury tore through him. If her brother hadn't gotten in the way, maybe he would have had a chance to explain. Forgetting for a moment they were in the parking lot of Safeway, he took a threatening stride toward Mason with every intention of kicking some ass.

Mason's posture and clenched fists indicated he was more than ready to have it out.

"Mommy," a young girl's voice carried over to them, halting Caleb in his tracks and making him look around. "Can we stop and get ice cream on the way home?"

Hell, the parking lot was full of women and children. He needed to tamp it down.

"Rosemary was devastated when you left, Caleb." Mason's tone now sounded more tired than angry.

Caleb lowered his head in defeat.

That didn't stop Mason from digging the knife in deeper. "You took her innocence, and I'm not just talking about her virginity, asshole."

So he knew that, too? Damn it, no wonder the guy hated him. He kind of hated himself right now. Caleb swiped a hand down his face. Yeah, he made a huge mistake when he'd walked away from Rosemary. Now it was time to make things right.

First, he had to figure out what the hell he was going to do about the job offer, and his career. Then he needed to find Rosie. He'd worry about making amends with his ex-best friend later. Only Rosie mattered right now.

Without another glance at Mason, he turned and strode from the parking lot.

As he walked away, Mason called out, "It took her years to put her life back together. If you care anything about her, you'll leave her the hell alone."

Caleb stopped, and for one heart-wrenching moment, he wondered if Mason was right. Maybe he should just keep on walking until he hit the bus stop, and continue out of town.

Then images of Rosemary's contented smile after he'd thoroughly made love to her, and the hero-worship shining from his son's eyes, filled his mind.

No, he didn't believe they'd be better off without him. He'd made the mistake of walking away from her once, and he wasn't going to do it again.

Slowly he reached for his Stetson and adjusted it before facing his ex-best pal. "I love her. Rosie and Carson are my world now, and I'm not walking away."

Mason's brows drew into a deep vee. "You say that now, Caleb, but we all know the rodeo's in your blood. How long will it be once your leg heals, before you take off again? Just cut your losses now and go, before Carson takes a worse hit than he's already going to. I remember what Rosemary went through when you put your career above her and Carson."

"That's not what—"

"Save it, Johnson. She's done with you. And once Rosie makes up her mind, there's no changing it."

Caleb's mouth set in a hard line. Mason's words held a ring of truth. Rosie'd always had a mile long stubborn streak that he'd found adorable.

But now wasn't the time for either of them to get stubborn. He was more than ready to meet her halfway or better.

He only hoped she could be persuaded to do the same.

"That no good, dirty, low-down, stinkin' cowboy," Susan hissed between gritted teeth. She stomped around her kitchen, throwing her hands up angrily, then shot a glance into the living room to make sure Carson couldn't hear them.

Rosemary snorted as she dabbed away tears. "Tell us how you really feel, Susie-Q."

Instead of driving home, where Caleb could easily find her, Rosemary had gone to her friend's house to hide out. Sitting at the kitchen table, she crumpled the damp tissue in her hand. Maybe by the time she decided to go home, he'd be gone. But as angry as she was, that thought still cut through her heart with the force of a chainsaw, leaving pain and destruction in its wake. Just like Caleb Johnson.

God. How could I let myself fall for him again? What a fool I am!

She'd never meant enough to Caleb for him to settle down. His career as a rodeo star meant more to him than she or his son ever would. Well, if he thought he could just waltz into town between rodeo gigs for a booty call, he was highly mistaken.

Rosemary glanced at her son, who was happily playing an Xbox game, with his headphones on. Fresh tears slid down her cheeks when she thought of how his daddy's absence would hurt him. *Damn you, Caleb Johnson!*

Susan stopped her angry pacing and came over to give her a hug. "You want me to send your brother over to break his other leg? He'd do it too, you know that."

Rosemary actually gave the idea a moment of thought, then released a humorless laugh. "No. I'm not wasting any more energy on him. It's my own fault, I should have learned my lesson the first time."

Her best friend pulled up a chair to plop down in front of her. "Honey, none of this is your fault. Caleb Johnson is one fine specimen of a man, and any woman would be hard-pressed to resist his considerable charms. So, give yourself a break. It's just too bad underneath that handsome exterior lies a slithering snake. You know, one of those venomous horned rattlers that can't be trusted near women or children."

At the apt description, amusement bubbled up inside Rosemary, helping to get her emotions under control. Susan was exactly right. She'd wasted enough tears her first time around with the Rodeo King, and she wouldn't shed one more damn drop. She had Carson to think about now. Her baby was going to need her when he learned Caleb was gone.

Yet she couldn't help but worry. "You're right, Susie. But how am I going to tell Carson his daddy left us?" That chainsaw took another swipe inside her chest.

"Lil' Tuff's resilient. And he loves you. He hasn't known Caleb all that long. He'll survive. He still has his uncle. You know Mason loves him like his own son. Why do you think he's been so crazy since Caleb came back into town? Your brother's scared shitless you and Carson were going to be hurt." Susan smiled sadly. "And unfortunately, he was right."

Rosemary swallowed against the fresh grief welling in her throat. *No more tears, damn it.* "Yeah. Unfortunately." She blew her nose a final time.

Susan stood, placing her hands on her slender hips. "Hey, you know what? I think we all need a vacation. How about we head over to the lake? We could rent a cottage for the weekend. Carson would love it."

Thankful to have such a wonderful friend to help soften the pain of losing Caleb, Rosemary nodded. "I think that's a great idea. But I'll need to stop by my place and pack a bag first."

Chapter Twelve

After downing half his beer, Caleb reached for the phone, got within a few inches of the damned thing, then clenched his hand into a fist and pulled back, letting it fall with a thud to the table in the kitchenette of his studio unit.

Damn it to hell and back. He stood and moved to the window, staring out blindly at the sun-dappled parking lot.

Three times he'd tried calling Rosemary's cell. The first call had gone to voicemail. So had the second. On the third she'd picked up, and he'd gotten out a fast, "Don't hang up, Rosie," before the disconnect beep clicked in his ear.

Stubborn, pigheaded woman.

Caleb raked his fingers through his hair, blowing out a harsh breath. He loved her so much he ached with it. He also knew damned well if she didn't want to take his calls, she wouldn't, regardless of how many times he hit the redial. His stomach knotted. He'd really fucked up this time. After earning back her trust, he'd destroyed it with one small hesitation, instead of giving her the answer she'd deserved immediately. That he loved her and Carson, and there was no way in hell he was leaving them. Ever.

But you didn't do that, dumbass.

Yesterday, knowing he risked having the door slammed in his face, he'd borrowed Nash's truck and drove to her house, hoping to talk to her. She hadn't been there. One of the neighbors, a busybody he remembered from his pre-rodeo days, informed him

Rosemary and 'that wild gal-pal of hers' had left for who-knew-where.

Since it was the peak of summer, and knowing Rosie, he figured they'd gone to the lake. So he'd spent several hours trolling up and down the road along Cruller Lake, a retired gravel pit the nearby town of Raymond had filled with water. No luck finding her car.

He'd finally given up and driven back to the Bronco Inn, stopping by the liquor store on the way. Damned if he'd eat his heart out any longer. Rosemary Carmichael more than lived up to her flaming red hair.

Memories of those silken strands tangled in his fingers as he kissed her, held her, made his body go tight with desire and his heart ache with longing.

Jesus, he missed her. Every tiny thing about her, including her temper.

Caleb limped back to the table and dropped into his chair. Hanging his head, he rested his forearms on the edge of the table, his half-empty beer no longer holding any appeal. Getting shit-faced on suds wasn't the answer, although a few days ago it'd seemed like a good idea. Which was why only eleven longneck bottles of amber remained in the fridge. He'd started with a case.

He rubbed at both eyes, then winced. "Son of a bitch!" Cupping his hand over his right eye, Caleb probed carefully. He didn't have to look in a mirror to know the damned thing was still swollen and probably colored a nice shade of purple. It throbbed like a mother, too. Mason Carmichael had a mean left hook. At least he hadn't socked the same side of Caleb's face, from the night he'd first hit town.

They'd gotten into it last night outside of DeeDee's, when Caleb stumbled through the doors just drunk enough to not give a damn, and demanded Mason tell him where Rosemary had gone. Two sore ribs and a black eye later, Caleb had staggered back to the motel and stocked up on ice, digging in his shaving kit for the ace bandage he'd used off and on as extra support for his ankle. After a shitty job of wrapping it around his ribs, he'd passed out half on and half off the bed.

Today he felt every ache, each fist-pound Mason had delivered, not to mention residual pain on his bruised knuckles from the punches he'd somehow managed to land on his hardheaded ex-buddy. Mason might have done more damage, but Caleb had left him with plenty to think about, including a nose that was most likely broken.

"Bastard deserved it," he said aloud, studying his ruined knuckles. He rose and grabbed the longneck, dumping the rest of it down the sink in the kitchenette. *No more beer.* He'd take a shower and go out for a burger, maybe hit that diner outside of Hawthorn and clear his head.

Except thinking about Hawthorn made him relive the hours leading up to the moment his life went to total shit. Groaning, Caleb sank back onto his chair and pushed his face in his palms, uncaring of the pain in his eye.

What was he going to do?

As if in response, his cell trilled. Thinking it might be Rosemary, Caleb grabbed for it.

"Yeah, hello!"

"Caleb Johnson? This is Lenny Folsom with the State Rodeo Commission. You spoke to one of my associates the other day. Bill Knowles."

He'd never felt less like talking rodeo in his entire life. "Yeah, that's right. Nice to hear from you, Mr. Folsom—"

"Oh, just call me Lenny. Listen, I understand you never gave Bill an answer about the job offer. It's a choice one, for sure. And something my team thinks you'd be great at, what with your knowledge and experience. Pays great, too. Did Bill mention the salary?"

Caleb rubbed his free hand over the back of his neck and tried to concentrate on something other than his mounting melancholy and images of Rosemary, naked and warm in his arms three mornings ago, before he lost everything that mattered to him. Which, he suddenly realized, did not encompass goddamn bull riding.

"I must be nuts," he mused softly.

"Beg pardon?" The voice in his ear—Lenny something-or-other—sounded perplexed and a bit irritated. "Mr. Johnson, have you made a decision? We need your answer. The current announcer is leaving next week. Retiring to Las Vegas with the wife and a thirty-foot fifth wheel. We'd need you in Cheyenne for initial training. Start you right on the circuit full time during the season, then rotating between our corporate offices off-season. Lots of great travel. We could offer you a spot on the board as a junior member and keep you in the loop. Full bennies, too." Lenny paused. Then added, "Mr. Johnson?"

"Yeah, I'm here." Caleb thought furiously. If he took this job he'd have to be guaranteed Rosemary and Carson could travel with him when he hit the road. He'd request his local base to be Cheyenne, an easy drive from Dustin. "Listen, Lenny. Can I ask you something? I got a family here. They'd have to be included in my travel allowance, and—"

"You? A family? Since when?" Lenny's voice held amazement. "I remember you on the circuit, Johnson. You were a tomcat."

"Not any longer," Caleb replied firmly. "I got a little boy. Five years old. And my girl's going to marry me soon." *I hope and pray.* "I have to do right by them and that includes not leaving them behind."

"Well, I don't know, son." Papers rattled in Caleb's ear. Then Lenny sighed. "Let me see what I can do. But you gotta understand, it's a big deal being offered a job like this. The Commission folks do want you but they make all the final decisions."

"I understand. And if I were a single guy I'd jump on it. But I can't be the only one who's got a family."

"Well, now, son, you might just be. You know how rodeo is. Damned few get themselves tied down."

Right about then, just as Caleb opened his mouth to refute Lenny Folsom's opinion, his cell beeped in with call waiting. He pulled it from his ear and glanced at the display in time to see Rosemary's number flash.

Holy shit.

"Mr. Folsom, I've got an urgent call to take." Caleb disconnected before the man could utter a single squawk, and hit the button. "Rosie? Rosie!"

A rapid beep sounded in his ear. She'd already hung up. "Damnfuck it!" His head ready to explode from the rush of emotion coursing through his body, he frantically pressed buttons. It went instantly to voicemail.

Frustrated beyond belief, Caleb let out an angry yell, then whirled around and pitched the phone across the room. Breathing heavily, and not feeling one damn bit better, he watched it bounce off the wall and skitter across the thin-carpeted floor.

Rosemary tucked her cell into her beach bag and stifled a sigh. Lifting her damp hair off her sweaty neck, she re-twisted the heavy curls and tightened the bright pink octopus clip that was supposed to secure the thick mass atop her head. When it flopped back over her shoulders, she yanked out what was left of the clip and stared at it. The spring mechanism was shot. "Ah, hell!" She tossed it aside.

"Now what?" Susan peered over the top of her sunglasses inquiringly. She sat up and reached for the bottle of suntan lotion they'd been sharing. "Here, make yourself useful and load me up."

"Well, turn around." As Susan presented her back, Rosemary slapped on lotion, rubbing it in with some of the aggression she was feeling, then rubbing harder when her best friend grumbled under her breath.

"Hold *still*," Rosemary snapped.

"You're taking off a layer of my freshly-tanned epidermis. Boy, you're mean when you're sex-deprived." Susan grabbed the lotion out of Rosemary's hand. "I'll do it myself."

"I'm not sex-deprived," she denied.

Liar.

"Pissed-off, then." With a smug look, Susan finished coating one arm. "Or just generally pissy." She waved the bottle toward the lake, shimmering under endless blue skies. Children shrieked in the distance; birds cawed above, and a light breeze took the edge off the summer heat. "It's gorgeous here, Rosie. Carson's having fun, you're wearing my sexiest bikini, and at least twenty guys have eyeballed you, most with their tongues hanging out. *Carpe Diem* and all that." She plopped on her stomach and stretched out, a sleek cat soaking up the afternoon rays. "So stop wallowing and enjoy."

"I'm *not* wallowing." Abruptly Rosemary stood, brushing sand off her arms and legs. "You can carp their diem for both of us."

She didn't want to be here. Even though she knew it was unfair to make Carson leave so soon, her heart wasn't in it. Turning slightly, she assured herself that her son still sat at the edge of the blanket with his trucks and sand pail.

Slathered in the highest SPF sunscreen available, wearing his uncle's 'go to hell' camo bush hat and bright green board shorts, Carson looked adorable. As always. He toyed with a plastic shovel, occasionally digging up sand and pouring it in his pail. He seemed to be having fun, and earlier she'd seen him splashing around with a few kids his age, but for the most part her boy was quiet. Too quiet. From the serious expression on his little face, she knew sooner or later he'd come out with it. And she'd bet money he'd start asking questions about his daddy.

Trouble was, Rosemary had no answers for him . . . or for herself.

She'd escaped town in a big, angry huff, refusing Caleb's phone calls, ignoring the voicemail he'd left on her cell. In the more sensible part of her brain she knew her attitude smacked of unfairness, but she couldn't help it. The man just scrambled her emotions. And all her insecurities had surged front and center as soon as he'd said 'Rodeo Commission.' Like waving a red flag before an enraged bull.

I never gave him a chance to explain anything. Not her most shining moment. Not very mature, either. So she'd given him a call, only to discover he wasn't answering his cell, and his voicemail wasn't engaging. She couldn't leave him a message. A hard lump formed in her throat along with a sense of *déjà vu* . . .

Because six years ago she didn't have a cell number for him, either. No way to let him know he was going to be a daddy. His folks had moved, their house sold to an elderly couple with a bunch of cats. Rosemary had no idea where the Johnsons had relocated.

How helpless she'd felt, sitting on the bed in her room with her parents silent and furious downstairs. She'd rocked back and forth on the edge of the mattress with her cell phone in one hand, pressing against her still-flat stomach with the other. Tears, so thick she could barely breathe, had dripped everywhere as she tried to plan out the most uncertain future she'd ever had to face. Seeing for herself how miserable her mama was, married to a man who didn't want to be tied down, Rosemary had made the decision to just let Caleb go.

"Rosie?"

She jerked out of her stupor. "Huh?"

While she'd been standing there with bad memories churning, staring depressingly out at the lake, Susan had sidled up beside her, and held out a chilled bottle of water. "Here. Drink some. Then I think we should head back to the cottage."

They'd rented one of the lakeside cottages, snaring a summer weekend special. The tiny three-room cabin was rustic but at least had running water and some semblance of power, although they'd popped a breaker twice when Susan had forgotten to shut off the coffeemaker before blow-drying her hair.

"I'm not thirsty." But Rosemary took the water anyway and drank a few gulps, wiping her mouth with the back of her hand.

Then gained Carson's attention as he raised his head to look around. "Come get a drink, honey."

Obediently he rose to take the bottle. "Are we leaving yet, Mommy?"

She ruffled his damp hair. "Are you ready to leave yet? We can stay a little longer before we go back to the cottage."

"No. I mean, are we going home yet?" His face was bright, touches of pink on his rounded cheeks despite all the sunscreen they'd used and the too-big hat shielding his face. He guzzled the rest of her water and then dug a chubby toe in the sand, a sweet little guy with something big on his mind. "I had lotsa fun, but I miss Daddy. I think he's lonely. I think we should go home and be with him."

Sudden, harsh tears formed in Rosemary's eyes as she looked from her son to Susan. He wanted his daddy. *God, I want his daddy, too.*

"Susie-Q, I'm just so lost." She didn't know what else to say.

Her best friend since grade school slipped her arm around her shoulders and squeezed. "He's a pretty good man, Rosie. Most of the time," she amended, tempering her words with a smile. "As much as I'd still like to just haul off and punch him for the crap he put you through, he's a damned good father. Whatever the RC wants with him, I wouldn't be surprised if Caleb's plotting to figure out how to bring you and Carson along." Susan offered another, tighter hug. "He's gotten me really mad several times in the past, but I think now you owe it to Lil' Tuff here to see what's what." She pulled the bush hat down to Carson's nose and made him grin.

While her son leaned against Susan's legs and yawned, Rosemary took a few moments to deal with the jumble of uncertainty swirling in her head.

Her brother persisted in painting Caleb as a bastard who wanted nothing more than an easy lay between rodeo hookups. Mason refused to see beyond his own anger. Despite the hurt Caleb's desertion caused her from years ago, still difficult for her to release completely, Rosemary had to see this through. Trust never came easy for her but maybe it was high time she grew up a bit and tried harder. If he broke her heart a second time, so be it. She'd lived through it once, she could do it again.

At least she had Carson. She glanced down at him, her heart filled with so much love that she ached with it. As long as she had her son, she could handle anything.

With that decision made, she began collecting their beach gear, folding towels; sorting through toys and empty containers of soda pop and water. Offering Susan a grateful smile for her support, Rosemary quietly said, "Let's go home, and see what's what."

Chapter Thirteen

Where could he be? Rosemary rapped her knuckles on Caleb's motel door again, then checked the painted number above the deadbolt. Fourteen. She definitely had the right room. Caleb had mentioned he was staying in Nash's studio unit, and the man only had one.

She was determined to have it out with Caleb once and for all. Was he staying or was he going? She had a right to know, damn it.

When there was still no answer, she glanced around the area and worried her bottom lip. The sinking sensation in her stomach grew as a sense of fresh panic set in. *Had he left?* Already gone back to the rodeo? She shivered at the chill rolling over her, stark against the airless, muggy evening.

Noticing a slit in the curtains, she peered inside and saw a perfectly made up room, with nothing lying around to indicate it was still occupied.

Gone. Again.

Tears threatened and she blinked them away. She wouldn't cry again over a man who didn't even care enough to say goodbye. Something she should be used to by now. Yet a fist squeezed her bruised heart.

Turning from the window, she spotted DeeDee's down the street and decided she needed a drink. After a final afternoon at the lake, Carson was spending the night with his uncle. Mason had promised to take him to the kid's matinee in Hawthorn tomorrow, which was playing the new Disney movie, and he wouldn't be home until late afternoon.

Plenty of time to get shit-faced if I want to.

Rosemary refused to spend the night alone wallowing in self-pity after being dumped again by that aggravating cowboy. Marching toward the bar entrance, she breathed deeply through her nose and tried to calm herself.

She dug through her purse for her phone and punched in Susan's number. "Hey, wanna meet me at DeeDee's for a drink and a bite to eat?"

"Sure," her friend said. "When?"

"Now." Rosemary pushed through the doors, scoping out a seat at the bar. It was early yet, and the supper crowd was just straggling in. "I'll order a pitcher of margaritas to get us started." Her voice sounded strained, even to her own ears.

"What's happened, Rosie?"

Her throat constricted as utter despair flooded her, then, shaking it off, she climbed onto the tall barstool. "I'll tell you when you get here." Her voice broke at the end.

"I'm on my way. Feel free to start without me. Sounds like you need it."

She hadn't even finished her first drink when Susan came flying through the door. She'd switched her shorts for a pair of tight jeans, but still wore the slinky summer top from the beach. Her hair was pulled back into a ponytail and she had a pissed-off expression on her pretty face.

Spotting Rosemary, she hurried over and took a seat next to her. As she poured herself a drink from the pitcher, she asked, "So, what'd Caleb do now?"

"He left," Rosemary said simply, sucking her drink dry through the colorful straw. She held out her glass for Susan to refill.

Her friend froze for a moment. "You're shitting me. Are you sure?"

"Yeah. Pretty sure." Rosemary clenched her jaw. Her first drink had taken the sharp edge off her sorrow, but it was still hard to think about being deserted again. And this time around Caleb knew about his son, but he'd still left. That hurt the worst.

Susan's gaze narrowed as she proceeded to fill Rosemary's margarita glass. "That dirty bastard," she muttered.

"Yep. That about sums it up. Doesn't matter. I'm done."

Susan lifted her drink in a toast. "Good."

They clinked glasses. Rosemary loved margaritas, and DeeDee's made the best, just the right hint of tequila exploding on her tongue. She'd skipped breakfast due to her nerves, and only munched on a handful of snacks during the day. Already feeling the effects of the alcohol, this would be her last one, at least until she got something in her stomach.

Susan abruptly straightened and glanced around the bar. An amused grin spread across her face. "Hottie alert." She nodded toward the pool tables. "Up for a game?" She wiggled her brows suggestively.

Rosemary eyed the two men at the back of the bar, playing pool. Both attractive and about their age, neither one of them looked like a damn cowboy. For a moment she was tempted, and when the taller of the two met her gaze, she didn't immediately turn away.

He smiled at her, but all she could see in her mind was Caleb's smile; the way his eyes shone with happiness, crinkling at the corners and lighting up his entire face. She'd been sure he cared for her, and wouldn't leave this time.

Boy, was I wrong.

Only when the man handed his cue stick to his friend and began walking their way did she realize she'd been staring, lost in thoughts of Caleb.

Her stomach sank.

Glancing back to Susan, she mumbled, "Oh shit."

Her friend chuckled. "Cute. Maybe he'll invite his friend over."

Rosemary snorted, taking another long pull on her drink. "Not interested."

"C'mon, Rosemary. Have a little fun. It'll do you good."

She shook her head. "Not tonight, Susie-Q."

Susan blew a raspberry. "You're no fun."

The man reached them, and Rosemary, unwilling to appear rude, gave him a weak smile. Her pain in the ass friend wasn't so hesitant. "Hi," Susan said in a flirty voice, lifting her drink in a welcoming salute. "I'm Susan, and this is Rosemary."

"I'm Brad." The smile he gave them was nice, but she still wasn't interested. "Did you ladies want to join us for a drink?" He nodded his head toward his friend who hung out by the pool table, watching them with interest.

"We'd love to," Susan chimed, grinning broadly.

"No." Rosemary shook her head. "I'm waiting for my boyfriend." She tried not to cringe at the lame excuse, but jutted her chin in defiance when Susan cast her an amused glance.

Disappointment flashed over the man's face, before he returned his attention to her best friend. "How about you, Susan? Ready to play?"

The innuendo behind his words evident, her friend chuckled. "Sorry," she said. "Raincheck?"

Just then the front door opened and Dave walked in, glancing toward the dining room. "There he is now." Rosemary hopped off the stool with her drink in her hand. "Susan, why don't you go ahead and play a game of pool while I have a talk with Dave."

"You sure?" Susan studied her intently.

She nodded. "I'm certain. We'll be in the dining room. Should I order something for you?"

"Yeah, I'll take a burger with the works." She returned her attention to Brad. "One game."

Brad nodded, offering her his arm. "One game." They turned and walked off together.

Spotting her, Dave came over. "Hi, darlin'. Where've you been hiding?"

Her cheeks heated. Dave knew damned well she'd spent the last week shacking up with Caleb. She drained her drink, before asking, "Have you had dinner?"

"No." He gave her an intense once-over. "Everything okay?"

"No. Not really."

Dave took her elbow and led her to the dining room. After holding her chair out, he sat across from her. "So, tell me."

Rosemary stared into his compassionate eyes and once again called herself every kind of fool for falling in love with a wandering cowboy instead of Dave. "Caleb took off again."

His expression turned dark. "What happened? Last I heard you two seemed to be working things out."

After Adrianne walked over and took their orders, Rosemary played with the stem of her glass, then shoved it aside. "He was offered a job with the Rodeo Commission, and evidently took it, because when I stopped by the motel to talk with him about it he was gone."

There was no keeping the tears from her voice, though she refused to let a single one fall. Dave reached over and placed his hand on hers where they were busy shredding one of the napkins.

"Did he tell you he was leaving?"

"No. He just left."

"How do you know, Rosie? You should have a talk with him before jumping to conclusions. I ran into Caleb a few days back, and he seemed pretty damn happy to be in your life and spending time with his son. I don't think he'd just throw that away."

"I tried, Dave. I went to the Bronco Inn, but he was gone. Not even a goodbye." Emotion clogged her throat.

"Do you love him?"

Rosemary frowned. "It doesn't matter if I do or not, because he left again. He left his son. How am I going to tell Carson his daddy is gone?"

"Do you want my advice, darlin'?" Before she had a chance to answer Dave continued, "I think you need to find out why Caleb left. He might have a perfectly good explanation." He sat back in his chair and picked up the drink Adrianne set before him. "It's obvious to everyone you're crazy about each other, so don't let your anger and insecurities get in the way. That's all I'm saying."

A flutter of hope sparked to life in her chest. Maybe she had jumped to conclusions. But still, she was hesitant to trust.

"What am I supposed to do, Dave? Just wait around until Caleb decides to mosey back into town again? I don't think so. I deserve better and so does Carson."

He gave her a steady look. "Then don't."

Rosemary just stared at him for a long moment, as the words sank into her brain. *Then don't.*

Slowly, she pulled her cell phone from her pocket, swiped it open and punched in a number. "Mason, can you keep Carson an extra day or two?"

She paused for a moment listening to her brother's voice, then quietly stressed, "It's important."

Chapter Fourteen

Caleb stood and respectfully tipped his hat. "Thanks, Lenny. For everything."

After an enthusiastic handshake, his new boss slapped him on the back. "We're glad to have you with us, son. You're bringing a world of experience to the RC as well as a fresh approach." Lenny shrugged into his suit coat and smoothed the careful comb-over that hid most of his bald spot.

The man wasn't fooling anyone with that hairstyle, and he probably knew it. Still, Lenny Folsom was a nice guy who'd bent over backward to assure Caleb had a future for him and his family.

Even if that family seemed out of reach right now.

"So." Lenny kept pace as Caleb edged toward the wide doors leading outside of the State Rodeo Commission offices. "When do you want to start? Not tryin' to rush you," he hastily assured as Caleb raised an eyebrow. "Just need a general idea for my team. That's all." He jingled loose coins in his pocket, squinting up at Caleb in the afternoon sun. "That little ranch on the outskirts of Cheyenne is almost ready for you. Your gal and the boy—Carson, right?—well, they can move in anytime, and—"

"I don't know about that. I still need to talk to Rosemary." Caleb was beginning to feel that rush Lenny had promised wasn't coming from him.

Surprise wreathed the older man's face as he stared at Caleb. "You didn't tell her? You're kidding, right?"

"I wish I were." Caleb rubbed at his forehead, feeling the tension brewing under his fingers. "I'll need to get back to you on that." *Shit, on a lot of things.* He wasn't about to admit he'd lost track of his woman. It was just a matter of location, because once he found her, he wouldn't be stupid enough to let her run off again.

"Well, if I were you, I'd let your lady know she's got a right nice place to call home once you start hittin' the road," Lenny advised. "Hell, I'll let the boys on the construction team know. They can slap on a fresh coat of paint, too. Whatever she wants."

"Let me actually talk to Rosemary first, okay? Then we can worry about paint." With another fast handshake and a jaunty salute, Caleb bid Lenny goodbye and headed toward the huge parking lot. He'd promised himself to return Nash's truck before four-thirty.

An hour later Caleb swerved to avoid yet another pot-hole. A repaving crew had been working on this section of 211, but it was a mess in spots. The back road was still the fastest way to get to Dustin. He recalled how many times he ridden the bus on this damned road, scraping up enough money to ride to Cheyenne and catch the summer rodeo circuit. He'd watch his heroes ride, and plot for the day he could be shooting his own eight seconds on the backside of the meanest bull in six counties.

And I did it, didn't I? Rode those bulls, made that fast money. Spent it, too.

For him it was never the horses, though he certainly enjoyed riding. It was always the bulls. And he couldn't regret a single competition during those crazy years. He didn't even regret the orneriest bull of all, breaking his leg in two places; laying him off bull riding, most likely permanently . . . because it also brought Rosemary back into his life. Carson, too. He'd spend the rest of his days thanking God for the second chance he'd been given.

When he bumped over that damned rut the county never seemed to bother fixing, Caleb knew he was eight miles from home. Reflexively he slowed to a crawl just as he caught a flash of chrome and color up ahead, sitting at an angle near the berm of the road. A familiar, dirt-streaked blue Civic.

He eased to a stop and killed the engine, squinting into the afternoon sun as he took in the sight before him.

Hot damn. God loves me after all.

Quietly, Caleb exited the truck, grabbing his hat from the seat and dropping it on his head. Leaving the door wide open, he stepped easy over road gravel so as not to startle the figure leaning into the open hood.

Shapely, long legs, covered in skintight, faded-out Levi's that were tucked into a pair of beat-up Dingos. One boot toe, squared off and scuffed, tapped impatiently in time with the sound of a hammer striking metal. Tendrils of smoke wafted from the vicinity of what was surely a dry and thirsty radiator.

He knew those red leather boots and those denim-clad legs; hell, he knew the heart-shaped ass attached to them. Rosemary Carmichael, love of his life, mother of his son.

Caleb felt himself slowing in anticipation, a dozen smooth opening lines bouncing in his head, a million things he wanted to say to Rosie starting with, 'I love you,' and ending with, 'Please never leave me.'

Instead, he walked up to the stranded car, grinning at the banging hammer mixed with a string of cuss words, and calmly—inanely—said, "Hi. Something wrong with your car?"

Cursing and pounding on the worthless piece-of-crap radiator, Rosemary never heard him approach until his low baritone voice flowed over her temper like a honey balm. Caleb Johnson, all six-feet-four of sex on a stick, sauntering over to her on those endless, muscled legs of his. He wore a pair of brown western-cut dress slacks, a white dress shirt with a "Hook 'Em" bolo tie, and polished Tony Lamas on his feet. He reached for his hat, a snappy, tan felt Stetson, and took it off, holding it in both hands, turning the brim around and around as if nervous.

Caleb, nervous? She'd never known the man to be anything but smooth and supremely cool. Confident. Bigger than life. Certainly not the hesitant man who stood before her with his heart in his eyes.

His heart's in his eyes. For me.

The hammer slipped out of her fingers and hit the dusty ground. She couldn't look away. Seconds eased into a minute or more as they stood two feet from each other and stared. Finally, Caleb's lips parted on a tender, yearning, "Rosie . . ."

"I was—I was coming to you." Tears blurred her vision; she didn't bother to hold them back. "I figured you must be in Cheyenne so I took the last of my checking account money and spent it on a full tank of gas. I was going to walk right up to you and tell you to come home."

While her mouth quivered over the words, Caleb had stepped closer and set his hat on the fender of her doornail-dead Honda. Now he used his thumbs to wipe her damp cheeks, his palms curving along her jaw. He bent in, the merest inch, and rasped, "Then what were you going to tell me?"

"I—I—" Overcome, she turned her face into his hand and trembled.

"Would it help if you knew what I wanted to tell you?" he whispered.

She nodded.

A single tug brought her into his arms and up against his heart. With a sigh she settled there, one hand grasping his shirt and the other sliding over his shoulder to bury itself in his hair. Caleb pressed his mouth to her ear.

"I wanted to tell you I found us a future together, Rosie. A job with good benefits and a chance to be together most of the year, living in Dustin if you want. Traveling the circuit in the summer with Carson."

He brought his lips to hers and touched them, so very gently. His voice lowered to an aching breath that feathered over her tongue. "We'd find a house with a yard. Maybe a dog. Maybe a little sissy or bro, too. And it all comes with a promise and a ring."

Dropping to one knee, Caleb held both her hands; she could feel the tremor in his fingers. "I don't have the ring, just yet. But I got the promise and it's so big and so true. Marry me, Rosemary Carmichael." He swallowed visibly, hard enough to cause his Adam's apple to shudder. "For the love of God and my sanity, Rosie. Please marry me."

How she managed to force anything out when her throat was so clogged with emotion, Rosemary never knew. But she choked out, "Yes, Caleb. Yes."

Three seconds later she fell into his arms, her senses filled with warm cotton and hot man, kneeling on the side of the road eight miles outside of Dustin, while cars zipped by and horns honked.

Epilogue

Rosemary gazed up at her new husband as they stepped outside the church where they'd exchanged their vows to love, honor, and cherish each other for the rest of their lives.

Her heart overflowed with happiness. The road to this quaint little chapel may have been rocky, but their future soared bright.

He stared back at her with so much love shining from his sexy green eyes, their son settled on his left hip. Caleb's right arm wrapped securely around her waist as he held her close to his side.

"Whaddaya say, Mrs. Johnson?" He grinned from ear to ear like a little boy who'd just been given his favorite treat. "Ready for that honeymoon?"

Carson clapped his hands, wiggling with excitement. "Yeah! I'm ready, Daddy. I'm ready!"

She smiled at her son, reaching out to ruffle his carrot top. "Mommy and Daddy will pick you up from Uncle Mason's first thing in the morning, sweetheart, then it's off to Disney World."

"Whoopee!" Carson yelled as they passed through the small crowd of friends and family lined up outside the church to blow soap bubbles at them. Spying his uncle, he exclaimed excitedly, "I'm going to Disney World." Then, "Auntie Susie, I'm going to Disney World."

Grinning, Mason held out his hand for a high-five as Carson passed by. "Way to go, Lil' Tuff."

Susan laughed. "I know, buddy. You're going to have a great time." She gave Rosemary a big hug, whispering in her ear, "Be happy, BFF. I've decided he's good for you." Pulling back, and putting on a fake scowl, she wagged her finger under Caleb's nose. "I'm watching you, Caleb Johnson, and I know where you live."

Mason punched the arm Caleb had curved around her shoulder, and growled, "Ditto."

Rosemary wasn't too sure her brother was joking, but Caleb just laughed it off.

Suddenly, a smacking sound rang out sharply, and everyone glanced toward the noise. A young blond woman was stalking off, and Dave Jamison stood there with his hand cupping a reddened cheek, watching her. A slow smile grew on his face.

Caleb stared. "Who's that?"

Rosemary laughed softly, wondering what the heck was going on. "That's Mimi's little sister, Dew."

Her new husband's mouth dropped as he set Carson down, then he snapped it shut and shot her a look of amazement. "That's *Do-you-wanna*?"

She scowled and punched him in the other arm. "The name's Dwana, and you know it. It's because several idiot boys who'll remain anonymous gave her so much grief in high school that she's changed hers to Dew. So use it."

Stepping closer, he leaned down and brushed a kiss across her mouth. "Sorry, baby." Then easing away, he glanced down at her feet. "Let me see those boots."

"These old things?" Lifting the hem of her handkerchief-edged gown, she showed off her beat-up Dingos, their silver-etched red leather vivid against the creamy lace.

His voice dropped lower, and he rumbled, "Damn, I love those things. You gonna wear them for me tonight?"

She shot him the sexy look she knew he loved best.

"Oh, yeah, cowboy," she purred. "Just the boots."

If you enjoyed RODEO KING an Amazon Review would be greatly appreciated. Authors LOVE reviews.

We'd like to share the introductory scene from our Award-Winning Novel, THE SUBSTITUTE WIFE, Book One in the *Brides of Little Creede Series*. Release Date May 9th, 2018

Chapter One

Chicago, Illinois

March, 1878

The earsplitting whistle made Retta Pierce choke up as she hugged her sister goodbye on the train platform. Jenny's slight frame trembled in her grip, and Retta fought back her worry.

Too thin. Too frail. Shoulders drooping, as though too heavy to hold up.

"There must be a better way, Jenny," Retta murmured, stricken. "It's just not right—"

Her sister's features took on that stubborn look Retta knew so well, indicating there'd be no changing her mind. "And what would be right, Retta? For Papa to really hurt you the next time he feels the urge to beat the devil from your soul? For him to finally slip and hit Addie?" Tipping up Retta's chin with two shaking fingers, she smiled gently. "That darling girl is the best thing that ever happened to this family, no matter how her skunk of a father ran off and left you."

Jenny glanced over to where their Aunt Millie stood under the metal portico, holding two-year-old Adeline in her arms. The desolate flapping of a loosened, rusty panel, noisily vibrating in the chilly breeze, only added to the solemnness of the day. Moisture gave a sad sheen to her aunt's eyes as she cuddled the toddler closer.

Retta's sigh was as broken as her heart. "No, of course not. But to leave you when you need me the most . . . Please, Jenny. Don't ask."

The dark circles around Jenny's blue eyes gave her complexion a grayish cast. She shouldn't be standing out in the wind like this, as sick as she was. She could barely stay upright. But Retta knew all too well her sister's inner core of strength, because Jenny was cut from the same cloth as their beloved mother, gone three years now. "Mama wouldn't want me to desert you," Retta began, only to be silenced by her sister's dismissive wave of one skeletal hand.

"Mama would do exactly what I'm doing." She shoved a wrinkled pouch into Retta's shabby reticule, ignoring her protests. "Take it. You think I would leave Mama's rubies to rot in Papa's strongbox?" She snorted weakly, but her disdain was evident. "It's your future, darling." Her voice dropped to a wisp. "It's my legacy to you."

Fighting back tears, Retta held on to her sister's fingers when she would have pulled away. "You can't go back. Papa will know you took Mama's necklace, and will beat you for it." She gripped her bag between whitened knuckles, then gasped at the clinking sound coming from within. "Are those coins? Jenny, where did you get them?"

Jenny drew herself up, straightening her shoulders, and for a shining moment Retta saw her sister as she'd been, before consumption ravaged her body. "My dowry. Yours, now." She patted the reticule in Retta's fist. "There's a letter folded inside with the coins. You take that letter to Harrison. It explains everything. Tell him I wish for him a happy life. Tell him I'm sorry."

She dashed wispy locks of dull-brown hair off her perspiring forehead. "I'm going to stay with Aunty until, well, until . . ." Her chin firmed. "I will be safe and well-cared for. By the time Papa sobers up enough to realize we both left him, it'll be too late to do anything about it."

A rambunctious boy bumped them as he sprinted across the wooden platform to keep up with his family. "Oh, Jenny," Retta murmured sadly, steadying her sister when she nearly lost her footing.

Retta blinked away fresh tears as Jenny gave her hand a final squeeze, before she eased away.

Aunt Millie transferred Retta's sleepy daughter into her arms then whispered in her ear, "I know, child. She wouldn't admit anything but I know how sick our Jenny is. I'm taking her back to

Dewfield with me. I promise you I will never say a thing to your father, and I'll care for her faithfully."

"You'll keep in touch? You'll write?" Retta clung to her aunt's vow, even as everything inside her demanded she remain to care for Jenny herself.

"Yes, indeed. Have no worries." Millie curled a supporting arm around Jenny's thin shoulders. "I'd best be getting you back to the house, darling girl. A nice cup of cocoa and a nap will do you wonders. Just you wait and see."

An errant tear tracked down Jenny's pale cheek that she quickly batted away before offering an encouraging smile. "Harrison is a good man, Retta. Be happy. All I want for you and Addie is to have a good life. Promise me you'll give him a chance."

Retta's stomach clenched with fear and uncertainty, even as she hesitantly agreed. For the love of her sister, she'd acquiesce to her final wish. Though it'd been four years since Jenny had last seen her fiancé. Who knew what kind of man he was now?

Jenny traced a slender finger down Retta's cheek. "I love you, little sister."

Blinking through a flood of tears that fell silently against the top of her sleeping daughter's head, Retta whispered, "I love you, Jenny. I'll hold you in my heart forever."

There were no final goodbyes, just an assortment of promises and encouraging murmurs, before Aunt Millie guided Jenny from the platform, toward a waiting hackney.

Struggling for composure, Retta held Addie close. As the March wind whipped around her ears, she watched them go until their figures merged into a single, blurred image, and the train whistle blew its final, 'All Aboard' warning. Only then did she allow the conductor to help her with her baggage.

Harrison had reserved a sleeper for Jenny, an extravagance to be sure, but safer for a woman traveling alone. *What will he do when I arrive instead?*

Blinking furiously, Retta guided Addie through the doorway. Inside the cramped compartment, she laid the sleepy child on the narrow bed and covered her with the only blanket she could find. Addie cuddled into a ball, snoring lightly. Retta brushed the tangled golden curls from her fair brow, trying to envision what sort of future awaited them out West.

Love for her child stiffened her spine. Her baby—her world.

I'll make a better life for you, I promise.

Even if she had to travel halfway across the country and marry a stranger to do it.

~~~~~~

Check out this and other stories at CiCi's Amazon page:
www.amazon.com/Cici-Cordelia/e/B01AJ5EM90

CiCi Cordelia is the pen name for the writing team of BFFs Char Chaffin and Cheryl Yeko.

Published authors in their own right, they share a love for well-written stories infused with their favorite romantic genres: paranormal, suspense, and erotica. Both are fans of Alpha Men and the women they'd lay down their lives for.

As a writing team, they bring a solid know-how for accomplishing the foundation of what makes a great romance read: a strong story, a passionate romance, fascinating characters, and a happy-ever-after ending.

CiCi can also be found at: https://ccromance.com & www.facebook.com/HeartfeltRomance

Individually they can be found here:

Cheryl Yeko:
Website: http://www.cherylyeko.com/ 'Where Love Always Wins'
Amazon: http://tinyurl.com/qzsks8q
Facebook: https://www.facebook.com/ProtectingRose
Twitter: https://twitter.com/cherylyeko
Pinterest: http://www.pinterest.com/cyeko/boards/
Goodreads:

http://www.goodreads.com/author/show/5406425.Cheryl_Yeko

Char Chaffin:
Website: http://char.chaffin.com 'Falling In Love is Only the Beginning'
Facebook: http://facebook.com/char.chaffin
Amazon: http://tinyurl.com/pvscu7w
Twitter: http://twitter.com/char_chaffin
Goodreads:
http://www.goodreads.com/author/show/5337737.Char_Chaffin

CPSIA information can be obtained
at www.ICGtesting.com
Printed in the USA
LVHW082300020320
648805LV00020B/1110